Mari smiled at him so trustingly that Russ's heart turned over.

If she was an impostor, she wasn't the only one. After all, *he* was pretending to be something he wasn't.

Russ wasn't what she thought he was—just a cowboy who was interested in her. *Interested* was putting it mildly, but the undercurrent of is-she-or-isn't-she-the-missing-heiress flowed continuously beneath the surface.

Gathering Mari to him, Russ impulsively covered her mouth with his, doing his best to put all he felt into the kiss.

Doing his best to bury his suspicions…

Dear Reader,

Around this time of year, everyone reflects on what it is that they're thankful for. For reader favorite Susan Mallery, the friendships she's made since becoming a writer have made a difference in her life. Bestselling author Sherryl Woods is thankful for the letters from readers—"It means so much to know that a particular story has touched someone's soul." And popular author Janis Reams Hudson is thankful "for the readers who spend their hard-earned money to buy my books."

I'm thankful to have such a talented group of writers in the Silhouette Special Edition line, and the authors appearing this month are no exception! In *Wrangling the Redhead* by Sherryl Woods, find out if the heroine's celebrity status gets in the way of true love.... Also don't miss *The Sheik and the Runaway Princess* by Susan Mallery, in which the Prince of Thieves kidnaps a princess…and simultaneously steals her heart!

When the heroine claims her late sister's child, she finds the child's guardian—and possibly the perfect man—in *Baby Be Mine* by Victoria Pade. And when a handsome horse breeder turns out to be a spy enlisted to expose the next heiress to the Haskell fortune, will he find an impostor or the real McCoy in *The Missing Heir* by Jane Toombs? In Ann Roth's *Father of the Year,* should this single dad keep his new nanny…or make her his wife? And the sparks fly when a man discovers his secret baby daughter left on his doorstep…which leads to a marriage of convenience in Janis Reams Hudson's *Daughter on His Doorstep.*

I hope you enjoy all these wonderful novels by some of the most talented authors in the genre. Best wishes to you and your family for a very happy and healthy Thanksgiving!

Best,

Karen Taylor Richman
Senior Editor

Please address questions and book requests to:
Silhouette Reader Service
U.S.: 3010 Walden Ave., P.O. Box 1325, Buffalo, NY 14269
Canadian: P.O. Box 609, Fort Erie, Ont. L2A 5X3

The Missing Heir

JANE TOOMBS

Silhouette®

SPECIAL EDITION™

Published by Silhouette Books

America's Publisher of Contemporary Romance

To Vickie Slavik, Milissa Anderson
and Christine Scheel—who love and work with horses.

 SILHOUETTE BOOKS

ISBN 0-373-24432-0

THE MISSING HEIR

Copyright © 2001 by Jane Toombs

This edition published by arrangement with Harlequin Books S.A.

Visit Silhouette at www.eHarlequin.com

Printed in U.S.A.

JANE TOOMBS

was born in California, raised in the upper peninsula of Michigan and has moved from New York to Nevada as a result of falling in love with the state and a Nevadan. Jane has five children, two stepchildren and seven grandchildren. Her interests include gardening, reading and knitting.

Dear Reader,

What ifs? are a writer's constant companion. One of mine was: What if a woman suddenly discovered those who'd raised her from a newborn hadn't told her the truth about her birth? This is how Marigold Crowley was born in my mind. I knew Mari had to be strong and resilient to handle such an unsettling surprise. I decided a loving but do-your-share ranch upbringing would give her the backbone to deal with the shock and, also, when the time came, to help her try to discover who she really was.

Because Mari never lost sight of her own integrity, she was a delight to write about as she not only navigated the chancy waters of legality, but at the same time had to sail carefully through the dangerous straits of learning about love.

Jane Toombs

Chapter One

Russ Simon hated what he was doing, but he knew he had no choice. None at all. As he turned the rental car off U.S. 395 onto a secondary black-top road, he thought again that it'd been a stroke of luck to spot that ad in the Big Nickel newspaper someone left at the Reno café where he'd had breakfast. "Draft mare for sale, fifteen hands high, all offers considered." After all, horses were his business. He fervently wished they were all that concerned him at the moment.

The May afternoon was warm, and the familiar scent of lilacs drifted in his open window, reminding him of his farm back east. So far he liked what he'd seen of northern Nevada. Good horse country. If things were different he just might consider buying some land around here.

When he rounded the next corner, the first mailbox he saw had Crowley Ranch lettered on the side, so he turned into the gravel driveway, heading for the blue-roofed house and stables set back among a clump of old cottonwood trees. As he neared the buildings, he looked around for the draft horse, but was distracted by a young rider who was winding an Arabian horse in and out among a series of barrels set up in the field next to the stables.

He was even more distracted when a young woman sitting on the top rail of the fence shouted, "Way to go, Yasmin!" She raised her broad-brimmed hat in a salute to the girl, revealing bright golden hair. Marigold Crowley, beyond a doubt. His quarry.

Russ pulled up beside the stable and left the car, sauntering over to the fence. "Am I speaking to the owner of the draft mare?" he asked.

Glancing at him, the woman nodded. "Be with you in a minute or two. Yasmin and I are almost finished with this session."

Her husky voice seemed to settle somewhere in

his bones as his gaze took in her delightfully trim figure. Watch it, Simon, he warned himself. This damn situation is complicated enough without you lusting after the woman.

Settling himself on the rail beside her, he forced his attention to the girl, who was riding what he realized was a truly magnificent Arabian gelding. Yasmin, who looked to be no older than six, handled the horse as though born in the saddle. If Ms. Crowley had trained the girl—her daughter?—then she was to be complimented on her teaching ability.

"You were almost perfect today," Marigold told Yasmin when she dismounted and started to lead the Arabian toward the stables. "Stan'll help you take care of Sheik. Then there's milk and cookies in the kitchen while you wait for your mother to pick you up."

Not her child, then, Russ thought. He jumped down from the rail and held a hand toward Marigold, but she smiled and slid off without his assistance. Were her eyes really the color of sherry or was he imagining it?

"So you came about the ad," she said.

"I did."

"Lucy's in the far paddock. This way."

Russ followed her, trying not to notice the enticing sway of her jean-clad butt. What the hell was wrong with him today? He could take or leave any woman, and this one was certainly off-limits. He lengthened his stride until he walked even with her.

"Lucy's sort of stubborn, but a real sweetie," Marigold said. "And smart. She learned the name I gave her in no time."

"You changed her name?"

Marigold favored him with another smile. "She was an estray, as we call them in Nevada, so I didn't know her name. I don't think she ever ran with a wild mustang herd, but she sure isn't from around here, because I placed an ad last year after she wandered by, and no one ever claimed her. I'd like to keep her." She sighed. "Unfortunately, she's expensive to feed and I really have no use for a draft horse."

He liked her friendliness and the candid way she spoke. Plus that sexy voice... Enough! He needed to remember why he was here.

"I'm Russ Simon," he said, "and I breed and raise draft horses for leasing."

"My name's Mari," she told him. "Mari— Crowley."

Had she hesitated briefly before saying her last name or had he imagined it?

"And there," she added, stopping to point, "is Lucy."

Russ wrenched his gaze from her and looked at the big mare in the field they'd come to.

"She's a dapple-gray, as you can see," Mari said, opening the gate.

Russ stared at the mare. It wasn't possible. He headed for the horse, unable to believe his eyes. After reaching Lucy, he crooned softly to her while he closely examined her color. "She's a Blue," he said finally.

Mari blinked. A Blue? What was he talking about? "Lucy looks gray to me."

He smiled at her and she blinked again. It hadn't escaped her that Russ was one of the best-looking men she'd ever met, with the most fascinating green eyes. As if that weren't enough, his smile was devastating. Plus, his jeans and shirt emphasized all the right places.

"I raise Blues," he told her. "The color distinction is subtle, but it's there."

Mari shrugged. "If you say so."

"I've been told the Blues descended from chargers used for jousting in the days of knights and fair maidens." He sketched a bow. "Were I a knight I'd ask for a token from you to wear."

Russ Simon was a charmer, and to her sorrow,

she'd learned all about his type two years ago. She'd do well to keep that in mind. Trying to deflect the warmth seeping through her from his admiring gaze, she said, "I've often wondered where the knights put those tokens, considering they were pretty well encased in armor. Are you interested in Lucy?"

"Definitely. Just let me take a closer look to see if I can figure out her age."

"From her teeth and the way she kicks up her heels when she feels like it, I'd say she's no more than five or six, so she'd make a good broodmare for you."

He nodded, his attention fixed on Lucy. By the time he finished his inspection of the mare, she was obviously entranced with him. No wonder, the way he stroked her in all the places a horse enjoyed, while he crooned softly to her. Mari couldn't clamp down on her imagination quickly enough to prevent her from wondering if he knew how to caress a woman in the same loving way.

Gritting her teeth, she forced her mind back to viewing him as a possible buyer rather than a possible lover—*that* she didn't need. What she did need desperately, was to sell Lucy before she ran out of money to feed her.

"I'll buy her," he said. "Name your price."

"I intended to ask five hundred."

"Out of the question. Lucy's worth at least a thousand. I'd consider her a bargain at that. If you'll keep her here for a while, I'll throw in three hundred more for board while I arrange to have her shipped to Michigan."

Mari did her best to conceal her surprised elation. "That seems more than fair. I'll be glad to board her until you're ready."

Russ glanced at the ridge of mountains to the west and took a deep breath. "That's sage I smell along with the lilacs, right?" At her nod, he added, "Do you happen to know if there's any land for sale around here? I came to Nevada to look for a place to start a second horse farm." He didn't look at her as he spoke, staring at the Sierras instead.

"Actually, there's an old ranch for sale just a few miles down the road from here."

He swung around to focus on her, those green eyes catching her gaze so that she couldn't move. Why was she so attracted to this man? Especially since she knew better than to get involved with another charmer.

"I'd ride over to look at that ranch if I had a horse a bit smaller than Lucy," he told her.

He did have a car, after all. She meant to agree

that Lucy certainly wasn't a riding horse, and leave it at that, but what emerged was, "I've got other horses besides Lucy. We could both saddle up. That way I can show you where the ranch is."

As he took her up on her offer, she told herself her impulsiveness didn't matter, since nothing would come of this anyway, considering how little time she had left before she had to leave Nevada. Actually, she had a dozen things to do before evening, but somehow she wanted to prolong her time with Lucy's new owner.

"We'll settle up first," he told her, and so she led him into the house.

Yasmin was gone. Mari shook her head; she hadn't even heard Linnea Zohir, a friend and neighbor, drive in to pick up her daughter. Willa Hawkins, though, was in the kitchen, and she eyed Russ assessingly. Aware that the old woman suspected he might be a boyfriend instead of a horse buyer, Mari straightened her out during the introductions since Willa, who'd moved to Nevada from New York two years ago, tended to be outspoken.

"So you bought Lucy," Willa said to him. "'Tis high time someone did. Mari takes in every stray that comes along."

And can't afford to. Willa didn't say the words, but Mari heard them just the same.

"Willa lives between here and the ranch you'll be looking at," Mari said to Russ.

"When I ain't fixing food for the Crowleys," Willa added. "Mari's uncle Stan is working on being the worst cook in Nevada, and she's too dang busy with all the ranch chores. So you're going to take a gander at the Curwith place, are you? Needs a mite of work, I'd say."

Later, the settling up done and the horses saddled—Mari had given him a horse named The Captain, while she rode her favorite mare, Tennille—she and Russ rode side by side along the verge of the secondary road in companionable silence for a time. Even though she was acutely aware of him, at the same time she couldn't remember when she'd felt so comfortable with a man who was a relative stranger. Quite possibly because he, too, was a horse person. Either you were or you weren't.

"So you live in Michigan," she said after a time.

"Near Lake Huron," he confirmed, glancing at her. "Great area, but I can see Nevada has its own charm."

He meant the mountains and the climate, she told herself firmly. His words had nothing to do with her. Even if they did, she couldn't afford to be interested. Not just because of where and what she was headed for this evening, but also because she wasn't ready to trust any man.

As Willa had advised after that fiasco with Danny Boy, "Best you take a recess from men while you sort out what you learned about them from him. Get things straight in your head afore you let another of them make-believe cowboys come snaking around. You gotta be sure you've figured out how to separate the poisonous ones from the harmless." Since she raised rattlers to milk their venom, Willa knew what she was talking about, whether she meant men or snakes.

"That's where Willa lives," Mari said, nodding her head toward the left. "She makes a good neighbor."

"I'll keep that in mind when I look over the place for sale. There's nothing like good neighbors." He smiled at her. "Especially ones who understand horses."

Mari said nothing, and not just because she didn't want to encourage him. Even had she wanted to, who knew what was going to happen to her life after this evening? Certainly she didn't.

And neither did Uncle Stan, for all he pretended to have no doubts at all. Why, oh why, hadn't he discussed the matter with her before sending off that letter to Joseph Haskell?

For that matter, why had she offered to show Russ this property? Because she'd wanted to prolong her time with him, obviously. Bad idea. Still, she wasn't sorry.

"How long have you lived in Nevada?" Russ asked after a time.

"All my life. Both in the state and on the ranch."

"Ever think of leaving?"

She blinked. "Why, no, not really." Which was true. "Why do you ask?"

"I've never gotten to know a real live Nevadan before." He hoped his words didn't sound as lame to her as they did to him. Back off, Simon.

Spotting the For Sale sign, he glanced around and, his gaze centered on a dwelling that had seen better days, said, "A genuine fixer-upper, no doubt about it."

"The barn's in fair shape, though." She pointed.

"Have any idea what they're asking?"

Mari shook her head. "Though since old Mrs.

Curwith died, I did hear her nephew was eager to unload the place.''

After they rode around the property, Russ told her, ''I'll keep it in mind.'' It wasn't a complete lie. If the price was right, he just might look into it, even though buying Nevada land had nothing to do with why he was here. This did look to be a good place to raise horses.

''Get out there and size up this latest claimant before old Joe does something he'll regret,'' Russ's father had urged. ''His ticker's in bad shape and he doesn't need another disappointment.''

Russ took a deep breath, moving his shoulders uneasily. Spying was not his vocation. Or his choice. Particularly since he was inclined to like Mari Crowley. But this was the first favor his father had asked since the schism had opened between them. The first contact, as a matter of fact.

''I've always liked the Curwith property,'' Mari said. ''I wish we had that little stream that runs through it. ''

''I noticed the stream.'' Realizing he sounded abrupt—the result of his distaste for his role—he turned to look into her amber eyes. Never mind how open and honest her gaze appeared, that meant nothing. When he found himself admiring how the tiny flecks of brown accentuated the gold color of her eyes, he shook himself mentally.

"I appreciate you taking the time to show me the ranch," he said, trying to sound properly grateful.

"It's the least I could do for someone who paid me double what I was asking for Lucy."

Waving that aside, he said, "To show my gratitude, I'd like you to have dinner with me tonight." Only to get to know her better, in order to evaluate how much of a schemer she was, he told himself.

When she smiled, he thought she meant to accept, but then her smile faded. "I'm leaving town this evening, so I can't."

His pang of disappointment vanished abruptly when he took in the full import of her words. Leaving town. Because his father hadn't been able to prevent Joe Haskell from inviting her to the island? Bad news.

"Later, perhaps," he managed to say.

She looked uncertain. "I don't think I'll be back right away. Probably not before you leave Nevada."

"Oh?" He tried to make the word an invitation to share a confidence with him.

Mari didn't answer for a moment. If she hadn't

been leaving, it still wouldn't be a good idea to go to dinner with Russ, even though she wanted to. As Willa would say, "Slow down, you're going too fast."

Best to end their acquaintance before she made the mistake of believing every word he said, as she'd done with Danny Boy. Before she had a chance to act on the attraction she felt arcing between them.

"I've enjoyed meeting you," she said. "It's always good to talk to a fellow horse lover."

"Yes."

Did he regret they had to part before they should have? Mari frowned. Where had that weird idea come from? Okay, so she knew. Because *she* regretted it. Because they ought to have had time to get to know each other. Maybe he wasn't the poisonous kind. As it was, she'd never find out.

While riding back to her place, Russ began to ask her about her childhood, making, she thought, idle conversation.

"My aunt Blanche died two years ago," Mari said. "She and Uncle Stan raised me, since my mother died when I was born."

"Your mother was your aunt's sister?"

She frowned at him, and he muttered, "Sorry,

I didn't mean to get so personal. I was just curious.''

Mari didn't explain any further. How could she when up until last week she'd thought her mother had, in fact, been her aunt's younger sister? She still hadn't gotten over the shock of what Uncle Stan had told her—that the woman who bore her had been no relation to Aunt Blanche. Mari didn't know who her parents were, not really. She didn't even know if this trip she was making to meet Mr. Haskell would give her the answer. Her mind was all jumbled with mixed hope and fear.

Finally pulling herself together, she said, a touch defensively, "I grew up very happily on the ranch." And she had. But, somehow, her uncle's news had tainted those years. Not that she blamed him. He believed he was telling her the truth when he said he was sure she was Joseph Haskell's granddaughter. But was it really the truth?

Taking a deep breath, she turned to Russ. "How about you? Did you grow up on a farm?"

He shook his head. "In a city."

"But you have a horse farm now?"

"It's something I always wanted, even as a boy. To raise horses."

"How wonderful to achieve your heart's desire."

His scowl surprised her. Surely what she'd said was harmless enough.

Evidently he'd taken note of her expression, because the scowl vanished and he said, "I'm glad I saw that ad for Lucy. Otherwise we might never have met."

She was on the verge of saying that if he bought the old ranch, maybe they'd meet again, but she stopped herself. How could she know what her life might be like in the future? "Yes," she replied simply.

Neither spoke again until they reached the stables and dismounted. Russ insisted on unsaddling and rubbing down his mount, and she didn't argue, aware she would have done the same had she been the visitor. Horses needed to be taken care of by their riders—it was the first lesson her students learned. Just the same, his caring for the gelding pleased her. Russ was not one of Willa's would-be cowboys. In her book, he was the real thing.

Eventually all the chores were done and, after washing up at the stable sink, they faced one another. *For the last time,* she told herself, unable to believe it was just as well. "Time to say goodbye." She tried to inject cheerfulness into the words.

He took her hands in his. "I'd rather it were till we meet again."

How warm his hands were. Warm and strong. Hers nestled inside his as though they belonged there. She could think of nothing to say. Certainly, "Don't go," didn't make an iota of sense. Especially since, in a matter of hours, she was really the one who would be leaving.

She drew in her breath when he raised her palms and brushed his lips across one, then the other before releasing her. Without another word he turned and strode to his car. Her hands clasped together as though to hold on to the feel of his lips, she watched him drive away until the car and even the dust plume behind it was no longer visible.

Chapter Two

Mari found Willa inside the ranch house, seated at the kitchen table pouring herself a cup of tea. "Looks like you could use some of this," Willa commented. "Get yourself a cup and sit you down."

Mari hesitated. She really should finish packing, but somehow she just didn't feel like it. Going to the mug tree, she lifted one off and joined Willa.

"Didn't look too poisonous, that young man," Willa said. "'Course, men ain't the same as snakes. None of 'em are completely harmless."

"He asked me to dinner. Naturally I refused."

Willa peered over the top of her cup at Mari. "Wanted to go, didn't you?"

"Whether I did or not, you know I couldn't." Mari set down her mug and leaned across the table toward the older woman. "Oh, Willa, am I doing the right thing? I'm so confused about all this."

"Seems like you got to go and find out, that's what I say."

"If only Uncle Stan had talked to me first."

"Once that man makes up his mind, he's not much for waiting around."

Mari sighed. "Or for asking anyone's opinion, either. It's just that everything has all happened so fast. I don't know Joseph Haskell. I never even heard of him until he came on TV to ask his long-lost daughter to come home."

"Stan sure enough thinks she was your mother. For all any of us know, she could've been."

"My mother could have been anybody!" Mari cried, blinking back tears. "I loved Aunt Blanche. Why didn't she ever tell me the truth—that my mother was some stranger she'd befriended?"

"I expect 'cause she got to fearing she might lose the baby she loved. Might be she and Stan couldn't't've adopted you if it got around there was no blood relationship. They weren't exactly spring chickens at the time. As for your uncle, he did what he thought best for you.''

''I suppose. But this may turn out to be a wild-goose chase. Maybe I ought to wait and see....'' Her words trailed off. Wait for what? Mr. Haskell's phone call to Uncle Stan had made it clear his present health was too poor for him to travel to Nevada, and that he was sending his private jet so Mari could fly to Mackinac Island to his summer cottage. This evening.

''If you don't go, you'll never know whether your mother was Isabel Haskell or not, will you?'' Wilma pointed out. ''Best you get to packing. And never mind that young man. If he's interested he'll show up again, and then you can decide if he's worth troubling yourself over.''

Show up again? Mari wondered as she headed for her bedroom. She wouldn't be here if he did, so a lot of good that'd do. Time to forget Russ Simon and concentrate on what else to toss in her suitcase. Although most of her clothes were for riding or casual wear, she figured she'd better take at least one dress and a pair of dressy sandals. She had to admit—she was scared to be going alone to a place she'd never been to meet a stranger who might be her grandfather.

Uncle Stan could hardly come with her, since he had to take care of the horses and other ranch animals. Willa might be spry for her age, but it was too much to ask her to do ranch work, and they couldn't afford to hire anyone else for the task. In fact, they were already one mortgage payment behind. The money Russ had paid for Lucy would help, but it was touch and go.

As for asking Willa to come with Mari, that wasn't possible, either. Willa couldn't take much time away from her own ranch because she supported herself by raising rattlesnakes, milking their venom and selling it to labs that made antivenin. No one wanted to snake-sit for her.

By the time the limo arrived to pick up Mari and take her to the Carson City Airport, she was ajangle with nerves. Twenty-seven-years old and she'd never ridden in a limo, much less a private jet. Maybe she ought to be feeling like Cinderella going to the ball, but she felt more like the untransformed cinder girl. If she'd been traveling as Mari Crowley, it wouldn't be this way. She'd always been confident in her ability to handle almost any situation. But she might no longer be a Crowley, she might be a Haskell, and that thought was unsettling.

Never mind, you're still Mari, she told herself

as she hugged Uncle Stan and Willa in farewell. You can cope. Once the chauffeur settled her inside the limo and they drove away from the ranch, though, the tears she'd fought gathered in her eyes.

When they reached the airport, Mari still wasn't sure she was doing the right thing. But her tears had dried by then and she allowed herself to be led by the chauffeur to where Mr. Haskell's jet waited on the tarmac. He helped her aboard. Inside, a uniformed man showed her how to fasten her seat belt, telling her he was George, the co-pilot, and introducing the pilot as Tom. George pointed out where she could find soft drinks and sandwiches once they were underway. It took her a minute to realize she was alone in the jet except for these two men.

As the plane took off, climbing quickly up and up, circling to the northeast, she closed her eyes, not wanting to see Carson City fade from sight below her. To distract herself from the disturbing realization that she was leaving everything familiar behind, she picked up a magazine from among several in a rack, but didn't open it. The cinder girl was heading for the castle without the benefit of a fairy godmother or a waiting prince.

Without Mari willing it, Russ Simon's face

flashed into her mind's eye. Her prince? The thought made her smile. Far-fetched as it seemed right now, maybe they'd meet again someday, as he'd said he hoped they would. She opened the magazine, Joseph Haskell's name popped out at her and she began to read the article about him. By the time the jet landed on Mackinac Island, Mari knew a lot more about her possible grandfather than she had before.

Since the article had stressed how wealthy he was, when she arrived by horse and buggy at the "summer cottage" he'd mentioned to Uncle Stan, Mari shouldn't have been surprised to find herself looking at what must be at least a fourteen-room Victorian mansion. But she was. Her jitters returned full force.

A trim, fortyish woman opened the door. "I'm Pauline Goodwin, the housekeeper, Ms. Crowley," she said.

Mari nodded as she was ushered in. "Please call me Mari. Is Mr. Haskell—?"

"An hour before you arrived, he was airlifted to Columbia Presbyterian Hospital in New York City. My orders are to make sure you settle in comfortably while he's gone."

"Oh, my, is he seriously ill?"

"We don't know when he'll be returning," Pauline said stiffly. "This way, please."

What kind of an answer was that? Mari wondered as she followed the housekeeper up a winding staircase. It must be his heart. He'd told Uncle Stan he had a "bum ticker." Whether he was her grandfather or not, she truly hoped he'd be all right.

The room she'd been given was decorated with white-painted wicker furniture, and paintings and photos of horses hung on the walls. Mari was looking at the paintings when Pauline said, "Frank will bring up your suitcases. Will there be anything else you need?"

As Mari thanked her and shook her head, she wished for something Pauline wouldn't have been able to provide. What she needed was a friend. Someone to talk to who she knew and trusted, someone who'd assure her she'd been right to come here. She worried how it might affect Mr. Haskell's health if it turned out they weren't related. The last thing she wanted to do was hurt him.

On TV he'd claimed he was a lonely and ill old man who regretted alienating his only child, Isabel. Mari had felt sorry for him, even though, at the time, she hadn't the slightest idea Stan was even then speculating that Isabel might have been her mother. Had she been?

I'd like to have a grandfather, Mari thought as she got ready for bed. I have no family at all except for Stan.

That was really why she'd come here—to find out if Mr. Haskell *was* family, a blood relation. It'd been a terrible shock when her uncle had confessed that Aunt Blanche had never told her the truth about her birth.

Though Mari had wondered if sleep would elude her, Mr. Sandman, as Willa would say, found her immediately, and she didn't wake until midmorning. The first thing she saw when her eyes opened was a photo on the wall of a dapple-gray pony with a small child on its back. She rose hurriedly to examine the photo at closer range, and saw the child was a boy. Not Isabel then.

By the time she'd dressed and was descending the stairs, Mari had begun wondering if dapple-gray ponies were ever called Blues. She shook her head. Probably not, since Russ had said his were descended from the huge chargers ridden by knights of old. If only she'd had more time to spend with Russ. How was it possible to miss a man you scarcely knew?

After a breakfast that made her feel she was

imposing on Mr. Haskell's staff, even though Pauline and Diana, the cook, were courteous enough, Mari escaped outside. Her uneasiness undoubtedly came from her own uncertainty—did she belong here or not?—rather than from the staff. But she began to relax a little once she set off to walk down toward the village.

May was definitely cool here on this island near the Straits of Mackinac, where the waters of Lake Huron and Lake Michigan met, and she was glad she'd worn a jacket. With only the clop of horses' hooves instead of the rush of motor traffic, Mackinac Island seemed not only peaceful, but somehow set back in time. In the gardens she passed, tulips were still in flower, though their season was long over in northern Nevada. Lilac blooms were tightly budded rather than scattering their sweetness into the air.

A passing bicyclist waved as he passed, and she waved back. What a marvelous vacation spot. She wished she could think of it as a vacation. It worried her that Mr. Haskell had decided to send for her instead of first making sure they were related by having blood and DNA tests done right there in Nevada. Why he hadn't was a question she couldn't answer.

She passed the Grand Hotel, staring in awe at

its unbelievably long and magnificent porch, and came into the downtown area of the village. Water gleamed ahead from what appeared to be a lakeside park. As she started across the street, someone took her arm, holding her back. She turned, startled, and gazed into Russ Simon's green eyes. Her pulse leaped.

"Mari, is it really you?" he asked.

"Russ!" she cried. "What are you doing here?"

He released her arm. "Checking my Blues. I lease twenty of them to carriage companies on the island. Didn't I tell you?"

Mari shook her head. "I mean, I knew you leased draft horses, but I didn't know where."

One of the numerous passersby jostled Mari, muttering an apology when Russ scowled at him. "Come on, let's find someplace less crowded. Place is already full of tourists and it's only May."

After they were seated at a harborside café, with mugs of coffee in front of them, he raised a questioning eyebrow. "Now you know why I'm here. Your turn."

Mari told herself to stop staring at him and start thinking. "I'm visiting the island," she equivocated, not wanting to lie and yet definitely not wanting to tell the whole truth.

Russ offered her his heart-melting smile. "My good luck."

No, mine, she thought. I wished for a friend and maybe, just maybe, here he is. On this strange island that seemed like another world, Russ was the known, the familiar. She might not decide to confide in him, but at least she now had someone she felt she could talk to if needed.

Russ took another swallow of coffee, trying not to watch Mari. Which was difficult because he enjoyed looking at her so much. Why the devil did her hair have to be molten gold and her eyes like fine sherry? Spying was bad enough, and it was ten times worse because he liked the way she smiled, the way she talked with her hands, the way she moved. Hell, even the way she sipped her coffee. No man in his right mind could avoid being attracted to her.

He couldn't afford to be, yet at the same time he needed to learn more about her in order to protect Joe Haskell. Since the old man was tough, he'd probably pull through this latest cardiac setback, but he didn't need any extra stress—such as an impostor on his doorstep.

"Like to go riding around the island?" Russ

asked. "I'll return the favor and find you a mount this time."

"Oh, yes!"

Damn, how could she seem so open and straightforward? The likelihood of a greedy, scheming heart beating under that attractive exterior was almost a sure bet, no matter how cleverly she concealed it. He knew all about pretty women and how they could fool a man—his ex-wife had taught him well.

Mari didn't have Denise's sophistication, nor did she wear designer originals. No doubt because she couldn't afford them. It'd been obvious that the Crowley ranch house could use some updating. Money was at the bottom of every scheme. He hadn't met her uncle, the man who'd contacted Joe in the first place, but it stood to reason that Mari had to be in on anything her uncle might be trying to promote.

Russ wished he didn't feel this odd bond between Mari and himself. It must be because of the horses. Unfortunately, that wasn't enough. They might be kindred spirits where horses were concerned, but just because she loved them didn't make her honest—and one Denise in a lifetime was more than enough.

Get to know Mari, yes, but hands off, Simon.

No romancing, no matter how appealing you find her.

"We'll ride first thing tomorrow morning," he said. "Right now I'm on my way to take a look at one of my Blues who's off his feed."

"Mind if I tag along? I know you told me Lucy is a Blue, but I'd like to see another."

He raised an eyebrow. "Don't trust my judgment?"

She slanted him a look. "When diagnosing horse ailments or in telling a Blue from a dapple-gray?"

"I can tell vet-visit-serious from layman-treatable. As for Blues—hey, lady, I'm the local expert, as you're about to find out. Be careful or you'll hear more about the breed than you care to know."

Damn, she was easy to be with. This was only the second time they'd met and he felt as if they'd known each other for years. Had to be the horse connection.

"What's his name?"

It took him a beat to realize she meant the ailing Blue. "Lancelot—the drivers call him Lance."

"Do you name them all after King Arthur's knights?"

"Used every one of them."

"I suppose you'll rename Lucy something like Elaine the Fair."

He shook his head. "Not when she already knows the name you gave her."

Her smile of approval warmed him.

After they'd been to the stable and found Lance already improving, Russ said, "I'll walk you back to—where you're staying." He'd nearly said Haskell's and hoped she hadn't picked up on the hesitation. But why should she suspect Russ Simon was a spy?

He knew some considered spying to be exciting and glamorous. Not him. He hated anything that wasn't aboveboard.

Mari looked away from him. "I'm not ready to go there just yet. I think I'll wander around and look at the shops for a while."

It was his cue to tell her he'd see her tomorrow and bow out, but instead he found himself saying, "Why not let an insider help you avoid the worst of the tourist traps?"

She hesitated a moment before replying, "Well, if you insist."

As they started back toward the main street, he said, "I'll buy you the very finest of Mackinac Island's famous fudge. This way."

"Why is it famous?"

"Ms. Crowley, you mean to tell me you never heard of Mackinac Island fudge?"

"Mr. Simon, this is a long way from Nevada."

Yes, he thought, just as a Crowley is a long way from being a Haskell.

Without letting her have a taste in the shop, he carried the white bag of fudge down to the park next to Lake Huron and steered her toward a bench, saying, "Your first bite needs to be savored while at rest so you can concentrate on the remarkable flavor." Only after they sat side by side did he open the bag, break off a piece and raise it to her lips.

When she opened her mouth, his fingers brushed her lower lip as he slid the chocolate inside. He drew his hand back quickly, disturbed by the tingle that ran through him from the brief contact.

Mari did her best to ignore the frisson his touch sent zinging along her nerves. She concentrated instead on the candy. "Umm, yes, it certainly does taste like fudge," she said.

He laughed. "One for your side."

She grinned, enjoying how relaxed she felt with him. "We're counting? I'll have to remember that. Actually, it's excellent fudge."

He dropped the bag onto her lap, saying, "Souvenir T-shirts next?"

Mari shook her head. Even if she'd wanted one, she couldn't afford to spend the money she had with her unnecessarily. Though she'd recently gotten a credit card strictly for emergencies, Stan didn't have any. When Mari was ten, Aunt Blanche had cut up the one she shared with Uncle Stan. Her words echoed down the years: *Gamblers got no business with that plastic. You go getting us any more in debt and we'll lose the ranch.*

Her uncle was no longer a high roller. Unless— and the thought chilled Mari—unless this entire Haskell business was no more than a scheme of his. A gamble. She shivered.

"Cold?" Russ asked.

"No." And, no, too, to that disquieting notion about Stan. Her uncle loved her; he wouldn't do anything like that to her. He might have been a gambler at one time, but he'd never been underhanded.

"The lake breeze isn't exactly warm," Russ said.

"I should be getting back," she told him. There might be word by now about Mr. Haskell's condition. She ought return to the cottage and find out.

"I'll walk you—" he began.

"No!" Realizing she'd blurted the word, she added, "I mean, I'd like to be by myself for a while. Thanks for the fudge. I'll meet you in the morning—where? Here in the park?"

His gaze was frankly assessing, but he didn't comment other than to say, "Remember where the stable was? I'll have our horses ready there. Nine?"

"Okay. See you then." The bag of fudge clutched in her hand, Mari strode away from the park, aware she was all but running, which was foolish. Still, she couldn't seem to slow down.

Running away from Russ when what she really wanted was to be with him? Yes, but did she want to share her story with him? She could hardly go on meeting him without admitting she was staying at the Haskell cottage. And why would she be doing that when the owner was in a New York hospital? If she was a family friend, wouldn't Russ expect her to be in New York at Mr. Haskell's bedside?

She hated to lie. In any case, she'd never been any good at making up believable ones. And, somehow, she didn't want to lie to Russ at all. Despite their short acquaintance he already felt like a friend.

And maybe a tad more?

Chapter Three

Walking down to the stables the next morning, Mari tried to feel optimistic about what Pauline had told her at breakfast. Mr. Haskell, it seemed, was "holding his own"—whatever that meant. At least he wasn't worse.

On such a fine morning, brisk, but with the promise of later warmth, it was difficult to feel anything but upbeat. Or was it actually because she was going riding with Russ? A bit of both, Mari told herself. It had been silly not to tell him where she was staying. Maybe he didn't even know Mr. Haskell. Still, after Mr. Haskell's dramatic appearance on TV, probably everyone did. Would Russ connect her with the missing Haskell daughter if she told him she was at the cottage?

Mari grimaced, disliking having to be secretive with a man she felt was a friend. Maybe she shouldn't worry about Russ knowing where she was staying. Besides, the island was so small he'd find out sooner or later, anyway. She might as well tell him herself if the chance came to bring it up casually.

Russ was waiting at the stables with two handsome chestnuts that looked like a matched pair. She tried to tell herself her heart wasn't racing at the sight of him, and gave him an offhand greeting. "Good-looking pair," she said, forcing her attention to the horses rather than on him.

"Same sire and dam," he told her. "My friend Nellis told me they were slated for one of the fancier two-horse surreys, but then Jill balked at having anything with wheels behind her, and Jack refused to be hitched unless Jill was beside him. Since they come from a long line of buggy horses, Nellis was surprised but happy when they turned out to be good riding horses. Genes don't always run true."

Mari blinked, unsure if the last few words might not somehow be directed at her. Almost immediately she decided she was way off the mark. He couldn't possibly know who she was or who she might be. He's talking about horses and nothing else, you worrier, you, she told herself.

To calm herself, she rubbed Jill's nose. "You're a smart mare," she said. "I wouldn't like one of those wheeled things rumbling at my heels, either."

"Just like women to stick together," Russ observed as he gave her a hand up onto Jill's back.

"I suppose men don't?" she countered.

"Independent to the core, all of us."

She rolled her eyes.

He mounted Jack, saying, "We'll ride around the island's perimeter this morning to give you an idea of its size. I'll save the historical spots and unusual rock formations for later trips. That is, if you'll be staying around for a few weeks."

"Uh, maybe." She hadn't a clue how long she'd be here. It depended on Mr. Haskell's health and how soon he might be able to return to the island. After that, who knew?

"Maybe you'll be here for a couple weeks, or maybe you'll put up with my company after today?" he asked.

Though very aware of how much she enjoyed being with him, she wasn't about to tell him that.

Slanting him a look, she said, "Both. How far is it around the island?"

"Eight and a half miles." Letting Jack set an easy pace, Russ led the way from the stables to the lake road that followed the island's perimeter.

Mari was charmed anew by the lack of motorized vehicles. "It's like living before they invented the automobile," she said as she pulled up even with him. "I can't get over how different it is here."

He gestured to the left, toward the arched span of the Mackinac Bridge, visible in the distance, connecting Michigan's Lower and Upper Peninsulas. "That's as close as cars get to the island. Except for a couple of emergency vehicles, there are none here."

Mari, watching a sailboat scud along Lake Huron and wishing again she was just a tourist, sighed.

Russ glanced at her. "Something wrong?"

She shook her head, not daring to dare tell him how troubled she felt over why she'd come here. Her birth mother had listed her name as Ida Grant on Mari's birth certificate. On TV, Mr. Haskell had given his daughter's name as Isabel and said she might be using Morrison as her last name. Why had Uncle Stan been so sure Ida Grant was

Isabel Haskell Morrison? As far as Mari knew, he had no real proof.

As the horses clopped along, Russ pointed out a limestone formation called Devil's Kitchen. "Not one of the more spectacular. We'll give it a miss." Farther on he gestured to a bluff on the right. "Lover's Leap."

"We have a few of those in the Sierras," she said. "I've always thought it strange anyone would want to die for love."

"You ever been in love?"

Had she? With Danny Boy? She'd been infatuated enough at the time, but after the breakup she'd certainly never considered leaping off a cliff because he was gone. Willa insisted her pride had suffered more than her heart. Whatever it was, Mari wouldn't make the same mistake again. "I don't know," she said finally. "How about you?"

He shrugged.

"So you don't know, either," she said. "I wonder how anyone can ever be sure about being in love?"

"Could be there's no such thing." Pointing again to the right, he said, "There's where the ill-fated Stonecliff ski hill fiasco was. Lost their shirts. The Island's not a popular winter resort."

In other words, enough talk about love. Which

was fine with her. Chemistry, now, that was different. How could she not believe in chemistry when just being with Russ gave her a high? But chemistry was definitely not love.

"Up a ways is where the British landed in the War of 1812 and took the island from the U.S. We'll stop for coffee at the snack shop there."

"You mean they captured that big fort on the hill overlooking the town?"

He glanced at her. "No matter how well fortified you think you are, remember there's always the sneak attack that comes from the direction you least expect."

Remember? Was he simply talking about the British landing or something else? His half smile made her think he might be warning her.

"I'll keep that in mind," she told him.

At the coffee shop, Russ studied her when she wasn't watching, acutely aware of her next to him sipping her latte. Sooner or later he was going to have to come to terms with his attraction to her.

"So in 1812 the British flag flew over the island," she said.

"Actually, the battle was in 1814, near the end of the war. After the peace treaty was signed they had to give the fort back to the U.S."

She stirred her latte. Without looking at him,

she said, "In other words, even a sneak attack may be only temporarily successful."

"Sometimes temporary is enough." She shot him a quick glance and he grinned at her. "All's fair, you know."

In love and war. The words he didn't say echoed in his mind. This sure wasn't love. Since spying was a part of war, you might call it that, though. Why not make a play for her instead of trying to deny what he wanted?

What was he, a male Mata Hari? Did he mean to get her in bed and then expect her to confess she was an impostor? Russ took a swallow of coffee as black as his thoughts.

"I don't think so," she said

He didn't have a clue what she meant, and his expression evidently told her so, because she added, "Maybe all's fair in war, but when it comes to love, it shouldn't be. Unfairness has no place there."

"Not everyone agrees with you," he said, thinking of Denise. Still, his ex-wife might never have loved him. He wasn't entirely certain she was capable of love. And how the hell had they got back onto the subject of love, anyway?

It was past time to get on with the spy game.

"If you're free for dinner tonight, why not have it with me?"

"Um, well, I'd like to, but—"

"You wouldn't condemn me to a meal alone, would you?"

Mari raised an eyebrow. "Poor you, all by your lonesome."

"You got it. Just me and my Blues."

"You could have worse company than horses."

"And better, too. Just tell me where to pick you up." He waited for her to hesitate, to try to wriggle out of telling him, as she had yesterday.

She surprised him. "I'm staying at the Haskell cottage. Do you know where the house is?"

He nodded. "How is Joe? I heard he was in the hospital."

"He's holding his own."

Russ decided not to push further at the moment. The last thing he needed was for her to get suspicious. His dad was going to try to get Joe to order a blood and DNA test on Mari before he came back to the island, but so far the doctors hadn't let Joe take any calls, even from his attorney, who was also his best friend. Once the tests were done, Russ's dad had little doubt they'd prove negative, which would mean Mari could be sent packing and not be around to upset Joe once he returned.

Which was fine. Except that Russ wanted her around awhile longer for his own purposes.

"Seven?" he asked.

She nodded, wondering what she was getting herself into. Riding with him was one thing, dinner another. On the other hand, why shouldn't she accept his invitation? What was wrong with being with a man she liked? She definitely didn't want to spend her time moping around the Haskell house, wondering if she belonged there. As for Mr. Haskell, whether he was her grandfather or not, there was nothing she could do for him other than hope and pray he recovered.

As they remounted and continued on around the island, she thought about Russ calling Mr. Haskell by his first name. That was more than she felt free to do. If she were certain he was her grandfather, she might be able to manage Grandpa Joe, but that had yet to be proved.

"Do you know Mr. Haskell well?" she asked.

"My father and he are friends. I've known Joe all my life."

Mari tried to think of a way to ask what he was like, but decided it was best not to. The magazine article she'd read on the plane had been a tad intimidating: "Gruff and forceful, Haskell knows his word is law."

Belatedly, she realized that if Russ knew him that well, he must know all about the search for Isabel. Did he suspect why Mari was staying at Haskell's place? If so, he didn't mention it for the remainder of the ride.

When they reached the stables, he said, "I'll take care of the horses."

She shook her head. "I rode Jill. She's my responsibility." Dismounting, she led the mare inside.

"What do you think of Mackinac so far?" Russ asked as they busied themselves unsaddling the horses.

"I do love Nevada," she said, "but this island is addictive. Sometimes I feel I'm lost in a time warp."

"Reality fades, yes. Can be dangerous."

She looked up to find herself trapped in his green gaze, making her want to reach out and touch him. Her breath caught as he took a step toward her. For a long, anticipatory moment she thought he meant to kiss her, but then Jack snorted and stamped a hoof and the spell was broken.

Dangerous? she asked herself. You bet your sweet patooties.

After they parted company, Mari decided to look into a few more of the shops before she returned to the house. Though she hadn't brought much money with her, maybe she could find a dress somewhat more casual than the only one she'd packed. Luckily, her sandals would go with anything. The last shop she went into before climbing the hill to the cottage had a sale rack. Though none of the dresses on it suited her, she found an inexpensive white skirt with a red belt that would look great with the multicolored sandals and one of the shirts she'd brought.

Arriving back at the house, Mari learned there'd been no word about Mr. Haskell's condition. She decided to take that as meaning he wasn't getting worse—a positive sign. Neither had there been any calls for her. Not that she'd expected Uncle Stan to call, but it would have been be reassuring to hear his voice. She thought about using her calling card and shook her head. There was nothing to report other than her day with Russ and the fact she was having dinner with him tonight. Her uncle wouldn't consider that news.

Since no one had told her she shouldn't wander around the house, she decided to take a tour, starting with the ground floor. She intended to visit the kitchen first, but was distracted when she passed what she took to be Mr. Haskell's study, where floor-to-ceiling bookcases lined two of the walls. In looking over the titles, she found one shelf devoted to old photograph albums, some bound in plush, others in leather. Some held yellowing photos of old Mackinac, which she examined with interest.

Over the fireplace was a portrait of a young woman who, because of the style of clothes she wore, Mari thought might be Mr. Haskell's wife, Yvonne, Isabel's mother. She'd learned from the magazine article that Yvonne had died when Isabel was ten. Peering at her own face in the long narrow mirror on the wall by the study door, she could see no resemblance to Yvonne. Mari didn't find any pictures of Isabel anywhere.

Turning to leave the study, she noticed Diana, the cook, standing in the hall beyond. "I was waiting to ask if you'd be in for dinner," the woman said.

"Oh, I'm sorry. I was on my way to the kitchen to tell you I'd be eating out." Deciding the cook might be a source of information, Mari said, "I wondered if there might be a portrait of Isabel Haskell somewhere, like the one of her mother in here.''

Diana glanced over her shoulder. Looking for the housekeeper? Mari asked herself, aware that Pauline could be intimidating. ''I'm not supposed to know anything,'' the cook said in a low tone. ''But I heard tell Mr. Haskell had her picture stored in the attic after she ran off to marry that rock drummer. They say Mort Morrison was pretty well-known, but you can't prove it by me. Anyway, Mr. Haskell's supposed to have burned all the photos of her. They had one in the papers from where she went to school.''

Mari had seen several newspaper photos of Isabel at age eighteen, with Morrison, but in each, her face was half-hidden by her hand, as though she didn't want to be recognized. In the school photo, taken with five other girls, Isabel looked to be about twelve. Her face wasn't clear enough in any of the pictures for Mari to decide one way or the other if they looked anything alike.

''After Mrs. Haskell died, they say little Isabel moped about for a long time,'' Diana continued. ''Her father was away a lot, a busy man, and she badly missed her mother. They were real close, everyone said.''

"How sad," Mari murmured. Poor Isabel. While Mari's own mother—could it have been Isabel?—had died when she was born, at least she'd had loving parents in Aunt Blanche and Uncle Stan.

"Yeah, it was that. Mr. Haskell had to raise her all by himself, and they didn't get on, by all accounts. They say he was kind of strict with her. Well, I got to get back and check on my pies."

After Diana was gone, Mari started for the stairs to the second floor, planning to see if she could find a way to climb to the attic. Did she belong in this family? Maybe if she could see that portrait of Isabel she might find some feature that had been passed down to her. Besides the hair. Mr. Haskell had said on TV that Isabel's hair was "an unusual shade of gold."

Mari fingered her own short curls. Aunt Blanche had always said she'd been named well, since her hair was close to the color of a marigold. Named well? Mari had never picked up on it before, but could Blanche have meant that her birth mother had named her? The thought gave her goose bumps.

Searching for the attic meant she had to open all the closed doors on the second floor. Since she'd already learned that Pauline's suite of rooms was on the ground floor and that Diana lived on the island, so didn't spend nights at the house, Mari didn't worry that she might be intruding.

Behind one door she saw what had to be Mr. Haskell's suite, surprisingly austere. Most of the other doors led to guest bedrooms except for one that proved to be the entrance to an upstairs sitting room. She ventured inside, toward French doors to a balcony looking out over the lake. Far below, one of the hydrofoils that ferried folks to the island swished past in a spume of spray that glistened in the late afternoon sun.

Behind the next to last door in the hallway, a winding staircase led upward. Mari peered up it and realized she'd found the way to the cupola, not the attic. She closed the door and tried the last one. Locked. It had to be to the attic. She sighed. Stymied, unless she got up the nerve to ask Pauline for a key.

Not today, Mari decided. It was after five and she still had to shower before dressing for dinner.

Later, after trying three different shirts with the skirt, Mari sat at the wicker vanity table, trying to decide if her red earrings were close enough in color to the red belt to be passable. She scowled at herself, annoyed because she'd taken so much time getting ready. What did it matter, when she wasn't certain she'd be staying on the island or how Russ felt? It was a sure bet he wasn't spending an hour and a half getting ready just to impress her.

He didn't need to. Though she'd only seen him in jeans so far, she knew he'd look just as good in anything he had on. Or didn't have on? She shook her head, warning herself not to get into that. Wasn't she in a precarious enough situation already?

Chapter Four

Mari remained upstairs until she heard the doorbell. As she started for the stairs, Pauline's voice floated up to her. "Why, hello there, Russ, how nice to see you."

He greeted the housekeeper, then asked after Joe Haskell. When Mari was halfway down the steps, he glanced up, saw her and smiled. "Pauline," he said, "I'm taking Mari to dinner."

Pauline's expression gave nothing away as she said, "I had no idea you two were acquainted."

"We're both horse people," Russ told her, as though that explained everything.

Pauline nodded. "Enjoy your dinner."

After they were outside, Mari said, "She's always courteous, but somehow she unnerves me."

"Who, Pauline? She's harmless."

"Maybe so, when you've known her as long as you must have." Mari paused to turn and look back at the house. "There must be a great view from the cupola," she said.

"Old Joe used to have a telescope up in that round room at the top. Is it still there?"

"I don't know."

"You mean you've never been up there? When I was a kid I spied on everything with that telescope, pretending I was watching for ore boats."

"I suppose you were actually watching girls."

"What else?" He handed her up into a one-horse buggy, got in beside her and clicked to the horse.

She'd already noticed he was wearing casual slacks with an olive polo shirt, the color turning his green eyes opaque. Unreadable. Which did nothing to alter his attractiveness. She could almost hear Willa warning her, "Handsome is as handsome does." But to date everything Russ had done qualified as handsome, as far as Mari was concerned.

"You clean up well," he told her, his gaze taking in everything from her sandals to her red earrings. "Nothing to spice up an evening like a buggy ride with a pretty girl beside you."

"This is my first buggy ride."

"I can guarantee it won't be your last."

He meant because she was on the island, she told herself, not anything more personal. She couldn't expect him to spend all his time with her.

As the horse clip-clopped down the hill toward town, Mari wished she could ask him about the Haskell family. He was too young to have been a contemporary of Isabel's, but he must have heard about her. But Mari feared to bring up the subject because he then might connect her stay at Joe Haskell's with the missing Isabel. What if she wasn't Isabel's daughter? What would he think of her then?

She'd come here expecting to meet the man who might be her grandfather and go through whatever tests he might wish her to have as proof that they were related. That would take maybe a week, she'd figured. But now everything was up in the air, leaving her in limbo.

"I do hope Mr. Haskell is soon well enough to come home," she said.

"We all do. Hope you like fish."

She blinked. "Fish?"

"My choice of restaurant for tonight serves the best Lake Superior whitefish I've ever eaten."

"I can't say I've ever tasted whitefish, but I do like fish in general."

They passed the Grand Hotel, all lit up for the evening, with carriages dropping folks off at the front. The men wore shirts, ties and jackets, she noted.

"I'll admit the Grand is the place for a grand occasion," he said, "but I prefer my favorite restaurant otherwise."

"By grand you mean like for a wedding reception?"

"Yes." His tone was so clipped she was taken aback.

Though aware he was scowling, Russ couldn't seem to stop. Since Denise's folks had had a summer place on the island at the time, that's where his and Denise's reception had been, with everyone stuffed into formal clothes. She'd lapped it up; he'd tolerated it. Maybe he should have realized then that they weren't compatible and never would be.

"Sorry," he muttered, aware he was being rude. "I'm glad you're a horse person."

He caught Mari's surprised glance and managed a grin. He'd spoken the truth. Even with this damn spy business between them, he felt more at ease with her than he ever had with Denise, who'd constantly chattered about shops and parties.

"I'm divorced," he blurted, surprising himself. He hadn't meant to lay that on Mari. "My ex-wife didn't want to live on a horse farm."

Which pretty much summed up the situation.

"She didn't know you raised horses?"

"I'd just passed my bar exam and was slotted to go into my father's law firm when we got married. When I bailed out to raise horses, Denise bailed out of the marriage." He paused, then added, "I suppose she figured I'd married her under false pretenses."

"But if she loved you—" Mari broke off. "None of my business."

She was right, it wasn't, but what she'd said was what he'd decided was true. Which had made him wonder if he'd ever loved Denise, either.

"That's down the river, under the bridge and over the dam," he said. "Tak's is just ahead, over there to your right."

"What do you do with the horse and buggy? I don't see any parking places."

"There'll be guys at the restaurant to return them to the stable—sort of like valet parking."

"How handy. I've noticed the whole island

seems to be neat and clean—considering that horses don't use bathrooms.''

''When the college kids come over every summer to work here, the new ones get the scut work of keeping the streets clean.''

Tak's was along the water, near the harbor. Russ ushered Mari inside, leading her to the booth that had been held for him. A woman came by and swept the Saved sign up as she greeted Russ. ''Be right back,'' she said.

''There was a sign out in front saying No Reservations,'' Mari observed.

''There aren't any—for off-islanders. Walt Takala and I were kids together. Lolly's his wife.''

''I meant to ask if you have a cottage here.''

''My dad does.'' Russ had no intention of telling her that this was the first time he'd stayed in his father's place in seven years. Other years he'd rented a room near the stables when he came over to the island to check on his Blues.

''Does he just live here in the summer, like Mr. Haskell?''

Russ nodded. ''Right now he's off island.''

During the course of dinner, he introduced Mari to both Walt and Lolly, getting a lift from the appreciative once-over his old friend gave Mari.

She was definitely something to look at, all in white except for a red belt and a decorative red stripe on her shirt collar, with heeled sandals setting off her long legs. And, for this evening, at least, she was his.

When they left the restaurant, the moon was up, three-quarters full. Russ tipped a valet to get them another horse and buggy, and while they waited, led Mari toward the planked pier, stopping short of it to lean on a rail.

"I can't get used to all this water," she said. "It's so different from the high desert in Nevada."

He made a noncommittal sound, his mind occupied with where to take her tonight. Not his father's house, no. And not to Joe's place, either. A drive in the buggy to a spot where they could look at the moon—that would be best. Slow and easy, he warned himself. Don't push it.

Once back in the buggy, Mari soon realized they weren't on their way back to Haskell's cottage. A tiny thrill of anticipation ran through her. Almost from the first moment they'd met, she'd wanted to know how it would feel to be in Russ's arms, and it looked as if tonight she had a good chance of finding out.

He halted the horses on a high spot, somewhere

near the middle of the island, she figured. Distant music drifted on the light breeze, a sad tune that lingered on the edge of her memory. Far below, the moon laid a path of silver across the lake. "If we could walk on water, I wonder where that moonlit path would lead us," she murmured.

"I prefer being right here," he said, putting an arm around her and drawing her close.

Her breath caught as his lips brushed hers, featherlight at first until they teased a response from her. Then the kiss deepened until they tasted each other, evoking a primal need from her very center. The little warning voice that cried *Too fast!* was overwhelmed by the warmth of his lips, by the silky feel of his hair under her fingers as she clung to him. The zing of attraction between them became a sizzle, threatening to turn her into someone other than Mari, turn her into a creature of passion fueled by this man's embrace.

She didn't want to stop, she couldn't stop; here was where she belonged. The night, the moon, the music were a perfect background for lovemaking. With Russ. Only with Russ. Slowly the identity of the tune penetrated her cocoon of desire until she finally recognized what she was hearing: "Danny Boy."

The realization was as effective as a pail of cold water.

Untangling herself from Russ, she sat up straight and said huskily, "I'd better go home." Not as positive a statement as she'd have liked, but all she could manage.

His voice was as hoarse as hers as he said, "You may be right."

Of course she was right. She'd suspected all along that being with Russ was dangerous, and now she was sure of it. Here she was on Mackinac Island, on what might be a false premise—who could tell? How could she possibly so much as contemplate getting involved with a man who knew Joe Haskell? That wouldn't do, not at all.

As Russ drove the buggy toward the Haskell cottage, he told himself he was glad she'd called a halt. He'd never dreamed kissing her would get out of control so fast, or that his need would take over so strongly that he'd had no intention of stopping. Whatever Mari was, impostor or not, he wanted her. Here and now. Which was impossible, given the circumstances. He could hardly quit seeing her, though, since he hadn't even begun to probe at why she thought she could convince Joe Haskell that she was his granddaughter.

"I'll give us a day to cool off," he said, earning an indignant glance. "But the next day, we're taking a private tour of the island."

"I don't think so."

"Why not? Don't you trust me?"

"No. I mean, yes, but—"

"You don't think we can behave?"

When she hesitated, he knew she'd give in.

"Bright and early the day after tomorrow I'll pick you up. Say eight o'clock?"

"Nine." Darn, now she'd committed herself. Which, if she were honest, she'd intended to do all along. As long as she and Russ were both on this island, she wouldn't be able to stand not seeing him.

When he halted the horse in front of the Haskell place, she climbed from the buggy before he could jump out and help her. He did get out, though, and walked with her to the front door, waiting until she opened it. Before she could decide whether she meant to let him kiss her goodnight or not, he bent and brushed his lips over hers.

"Sweet dreams," he murmured.

Inside, she leaned against the closed door for a moment. She'd never met a man quite like Russ. Maybe there *were* no other men like him. Once in bed, she began to relive the moments in his arms. No matter how firmly she muttered, "Chemistry," she didn't convince herself. Russ transported her beyond herself in a way she'd never before experienced. Mere chemistry didn't begin to cover how he made her feel.

Her dreams were definitely not sweet.

In the morning she faced a day without seeing Russ, and felt oddly depressed. While she was eating breakfast, Pauline, to her surprise, sat down at the table and poured herself a cup of coffee.

"Mr. Haskell's doctors are optimistic," she told Mari. "They hope to move him out of the cardiac care unit in a day or two."

"That's good news."

"Oh, yes. Both Diana and I are very fond of him."

Since Mari could hardly say she was, too, she remained silent.

After a moment Pauline said, "Russ Simon is a decent enough young man."

Not clear where this was headed, Mari murmured, "Uh, yes, he seems to be."

"His father flew to New York to be with Mr. Haskell, you know."

"Russ mentioned they were friends."

"The elder Mr. Simon is also Mr. Haskell's attorney."

Was Pauline warning her? If so, Mari wasn't altogether sure what about. It stood to reason Mr. Haskell would want a friend to be his attorney. Not for the first time Mari wondered if the housekeeper knew or suspected why she was here. Well, whether she did or not, since Pauline had taken the initiative of joining her at the table, this might be the best time to broach the subject of the locked attic door.

"I hope you don't mind how I've been roaming around the house," Mari began.

"Of course not."

"I did happen to notice one of the upstairs doors was locked, and it made me curious. Is that the way to the attic?"

"Why, yes, we keep it locked. So much is stored up there. The place is jam-packed with valuables."

Valuables. Mari's heart sank. No way did she want the responsibility of having a key to where valuables were stored. But she wasn't ready to give up. "The reason I asked was that I noticed the beautiful portrait in the study, and thought there might be some other old family portraits stored away."

Pauline shook her head. "Mr. Haskell keeps those in a special room at his house in Grand Rapids." She smiled slightly. "He brings his wife's picture with him when he comes to the island. We find it endearing that he doesn't want to leave her behind."

It *was* endearing. Maybe this man who might be her grandfather wasn't as formidable as Mari pictured him.

Giving it one last try, she said, "So there are no family pictures in the attic."

"Not a one." The housekeeper gave her a knowing look. "You must have been talking to Diana. She's convinced Mr. Haskell stored a portrait of his daughter up there, but she's wrong. I inventory the attic contents each spring and there is no such portrait among them."

So much for that idea.

"Will you be here for lunch and dinner today?" Pauline asked.

Mari nodded. She didn't have anything planned other than maybe taking a walk over to look at the old fort.

Later, as she was wandering around the grounds of Fort Mackinac, viewing the remains of barracks, storerooms and some formidable-looking cannons, Pauline's words returned to plague her. Why had the housekeeper bothered to tell her Russ's father was Mr. Haskell's attorney? Pauline didn't seem the type for idle chatter. She'd mentioned Russ, too. "Decent enough?" A chill trickled through Mari. Was it mere coincidence that Russ had first showed up at her ranch in Nevada, then here on Mackinac Island?

After a moment she shook her head. Russ had flown to Nevada to look for land for a second horse ranch. He'd happened to see her ad for a draft horse, so came to look at Lucy and had been thrilled to find out the mare was a Blue. As for this island—he came here every summer to keep an eye on the Blues he leased to the carriage tour company. He'd had a perfectly valid reason for being in Nevada as well as here. So, okay, his father was Mr. Haskell's attorney. But Russ wasn't. He raised horses. Like she did. They were horse people.

What had seemed a good idea last evening to Russ—keep away from Mari for a day and a night—didn't much appeal to him as the day dragged on. Ordinarily, time passed fast when he was working with his horses, but not today. He couldn't erase the feel of her in his arms or her unabashed response to his kiss. If something hadn't spooked her, they might well have made love right there in the damn buggy.

If they had, would he still be so turned on by the mere thought of her?

He shook his head. A buggy wasn't the best place for lovemaking. What had he been thinking of? The truth was, once he kissed her, he hadn't been capable of thinking. No other woman had ever affected him so acutely. Those sherry-colored eyes of hers were as intoxicating as the wine they resembled.

Denise had been fond of expensive perfumes. He didn't particularly care for them and couldn't so much as recall which had been her favorite or whether it had been sweet or spicy. Mari, though, used scent so sparingly he hadn't been aware of any until she was in his arms. Then the faint smell of lilacs seemed to be a part of her own personal scent, one he longed to experience again. Soon. Right now, as a matter of fact. He sighed.

"Something bugging you, Russ?" Ken, one of the carriage drivers, asked.

Russ blinked, having forgotten anyone was around. "Bugging me? Why?"

"For one thing, you been grooming the same spot on Lance for the last five minutes."

"Wasn't thinking," Russ muttered

"Wasn't paying attention, that's for sure. Reminds me of them college guys when they get to mooning over one of the gals."

Russ scowled at him and Ken grinned, revealing two gold teeth.

"Gotcha, hey?"

Shrugging, Russ turned his attention to finishing the grooming of his Blue gelding, his mind made up to keep Mari out of his head for the rest of the day.

Which he managed to do, more or less, until he climbed into bed that night. Even then, he confined his thoughts of her to how, without tipping his hand, he might manage tomorrow to bring the conversation around to Joe Haskell's search for Isabel. Wasn't that his primary purpose, after all? To get her talking about why she was at Haskell's and what she'd done to get here?

Then he slept, and Mari was featured in every damn erotic dream.

Chapter Five

Mari leaned on the rail of the balcony of the upstairs sitting room, gazing at the morning sun glinting on the lake. Another beautiful day, though cooler than May in Nevada. Tomorrow would be June 1—surely the lilacs would begin to bloom here by then. Today, though, was the important one, and it was almost nine o'clock. Hearing the clip-clop of hooves, she ducked back into the sitting room, grabbed her jacket off a chair and flew downstairs.

Diana was in the entry. She held out what was obviously a picnic basket to Mari, saying, "Pauline told me you were touring the island today and wouldn't be back for lunch. So I fixed you and Russ a picnic. He's always liked my cooking.''

Nothing was a secret on this island, Mari thought ruefully as she took the basket. She hadn't actually told Pauline she'd be with Russ, but the housekeeper was one step ahead of her.

''That's wonderful, Diana,'' she said. ''Thanks.''

The doorbell rang. Diana opened the door and greeted Russ. ''Fixed the two of you a picnic lunch,'' she said.

Russ gave her a hug. ''You're my favorite cook, bar none. ''

Diana beamed and then stood in the doorway to watch them off. From the buggy, Mari looked back at her and waved.

''Your name is like a magic wand,'' she told Russ. ''Pauline has thawed at least halfway and Diana is now making special treats for me.''

''We islanders are kind of clannish,'' he said. ''Even those families who only live here in the summer count as islanders, provided at least two generations have been coming. Three's even better. Everyone else is a tourist.''

Like me, Mari thought, only she wasn't, not really. She wouldn't be here if Mr. Haskell hadn't sent for her. And he wouldn't have sent for her, would he, if he didn't think she might be Isabel's daughter? It always came back to that. Was she or wasn't she?

"Thought we'd stop by for a look up Robinson's Folly first." Russ said. "Actually, his name was Robertson, but you know what myths are like."

Mari brought her attention back to the moment. "What folly did Robertson-Robinson commit that turned him into a myth?"

"Fact. Captain Daniel Robertson was the commander of the fort in the early 1780s. He may have built a house on the bluff too close to the edge, a house that was destroyed when part of the cliff crumbled away. This could be true, since an 1822 guidebook mentioned the debris could still be seen on the beach below."

"That doesn't sound mythlike."

"It's only theory number one. The rest all involve beautiful maidens and vengeful warriors, and some end with Robertson's death on the rocks below the bluff. The truth is he left Mackinac Island very much alive in the late 1780s."

"So the fact is he did exist and may have built a house on the bluff that may have slid down the side of the cliff."

They rounded a corner, and Russ eased the buggy off the road, stopped the horse and gestured to the left. Mari stared up at a limestone cliff rising a hundred or so feet above them.

"I don't know," she said at last. "To me a folly is doing something daring, even though in your heart you know it may be foolish of you."

"You'd prefer one of the maiden and warrior myths?"

"Maybe he couldn't help loving the maiden even though it wasn't wise."

"What about her—did she love him?"

"Oh, yes. It probably wasn't wise of her, either."

"In other words, a doomed love."

"In myths it's usually that way."

"But does it have to be?"

She had no answer.

He clucked to the horse and pulled back onto the road. "Next stop, Arch Rock."

"Are there multiple myths connected with it, too?"

"Just one." He told it to her as they drove on.

When they reached Arch Rock, a tour carriage was just leaving, all the tourists aboard it. "Good," Russ said as they got down from the buggy. "We have the place to ourselves except for the birds and the bats."

Mari glanced around. "Bats?"

"They're asleep at the moment. See those holes?"

She noticed hundreds of small openings in the pitted limestone that formed the impressive rock bridge arching over emptiness.

"Bats nest inside the holes in the limestone. Since the entire island is limestone based, and limestone tends to be full of holes, we've lots of bats."

So, okay, bats ate mosquitoes, which was good. Enough about them. Looking up at the rock arch, she thought about the Native American myth Russ had told her—the maiden whose cruel father wouldn't allow her to marry the warrior she loved, and punished her by tying her to the arch until she promised to give up her folly. Another case of doomed love? No, because the warrior, being one of the Sky People, waited until the Evening Star rose and descended on its rays to rescue her and bear her back to his people in the sky.

Mari sighed. "I like happy endings."

Russ shrugged. "Who doesn't?"

"I was thinking about the Evening Star myth,

one that *did* have a happy ending. Maybe some version of it actually did happen.''

''Evening Star and all?''

''That's so romantic. It could be the warrior rescued her by the light of the star.''

He smiled. ''If you say so.'' He took her hand and led her back to the buggy. ''Next you can tell me what you think of my choice of a picnic spot.''

With her hand nestled warmly in his, Mari, who had never been a fearful or dependent person, suddenly felt safe and protected. Unsure whether she wanted to accept the feeling or not, she tugged her hand free, saying, ''You're hungry already?''

Grinning at her, he said, ''For many things.''

They rode for some time, heading into a thickly wooded area, where he finally turned off onto what was scarcely a trail. ''Have to leave the buggy and walk the rest of the way in,'' he told her when the trees began to grow too close to permit passage.

He lifted a blanket off the buggy seat and, carrying it with the picnic basket, led the way among the trees until they came into a small grassy clearing. Stopping, he turned to her. ''Romantic enough for you?''

''If you say so,'' she mocked.

Laughing, he set down the basket and flung the blanket over the grass. With a bow, he invited her to sit.

Diana's choice of picnic food was not exotic—sandwiches, cookies and bottled water—but the bread was homemade, as were the sandwich fillings, and her ginger cookies were to die for.

"Diana and Pauline seem very fond of Mr. Haskell," Mari said when they'd finished eating and stowed the remainders back inside the basket.

"Joe's mellowed a lot."

"I understand your father is his attorney."

Russ would lay odds she'd heard that from Pauline. "And his friend. My father called me this morning to say they're moving Joe out of the cardiac care unit today. My dad's been acting as family, since Joe doesn't really have any."

"I'm glad someone is there with him."

Russ didn't comment, waiting to see if she'd make some excuse for not being there herself.

She fidgeted, then changed position on the blanket, sitting straighter and clasping her hands around her jean-clad knees. He continued to wait.

"I'd be there with him," she said finally, "if I could be sure I had the right to be."

"I don't understand." A barefaced lie, but he

could hardly admit to the truth—that he knew exactly why she was on the island.

She shifted around until she was facing away from him. "You know about Mr. Haskell asking on TV for his daughter Isabel to come home."

"Yes."

"Well, my uncle Stan got to thinking about my birth mother." She glanced at Russ, then away. "You see, after my aunt Blanche and he adopted me, they got my birth certificate changed so they were listed as my parents. That's the one I always used when I had to show one. I knew they weren't my birth parents, but I didn't think about that—they were the only family I'd ever had." She took a deep breath and let it out in a sigh.

"My uncle got out my original birth certificate, where my birth parents are listed, and he wondered if the Ida Grant who gave birth to me might not be Isabel Haskell. You see, he remembered my aunt Blanche telling him Ida had the same color hair as I do, the color Mr. Haskell mentioned on TV. My aunt died two years ago or she might have argued with him about what he did next, I don't know. Anyway, he made a copy of the birth certificate and wrote a letter," after a moment she added, "my uncle has always been a gambler and so I guess he convinced himself Isabel was my birth mother.''

She paused. Russ said nothing, afraid if he made any comment, she might not continue.

Swiveling to face him, Mari said, ''My aunt Blanche was a blackjack dealer in one of the big Reno casinos. One day she went into the woman's bathroom on her break and found this poor, sick and pregnant woman leaning against the wall crying. My aunt was always bringing strays home— dogs, cats, a goat and once a llama. So she took Ida Grant to the hospital and stayed with her while the baby was born—me. My birth mother lived only a few hours after I was born, long enough for her to sign papers listing Blanche Crowley as next of kin and my guardian.''

Running her hand over her forehead, Mari sighed. ''I always thought Blanche really was my aunt. It wasn't until Uncle Stan decided Ida must be Isabel that he told me the truth. Blanche was no relation to Ida, so no blood relation to me. But this was after he sent the birth certificate copy, my picture and the letter he wrote explaining his theory to Mr. Haskell. I wasn't consulted beforehand.''

Russ thought this over. ''You're saying you didn't know your uncle had contacted Joe?''

"Not until Uncle Stan got the phone call from Mr. Haskell inviting me to come here. I was really upset at first and meant to refuse to go. But then I couldn't help but wonder who I really was. Could I be a Haskell? As Willa told me, if I didn't go I'd never find out. And then there was Mr. Haskell—old and ailing. If it was possible I was his granddaughter, was it fair to him for me to refuse to come here?" She spread her hands. "I'm still not sure I did the right thing."

Mari was damn convincing, Russ had to give her that. Still, he was none too sure any woman could be as straightforward as she made herself sound.

"Do you think my decision is so very terrible?" she asked. "I'd hate to hurt Mr. Haskell."

Russ cleared his throat. His father had told him that he was going to ask Joe as soon as he improved if, as Joe's lawyer, he could arrange to have blood and DNA tests done on Mari. His dad felt it was important to get the tests done before Joe was well enough to return to the island. If Mari was an impostor, then she'd be long gone and not around to upset the old man.

"I should think that Joe would arrange for tests to be done to confirm whether or not you are a

Haskell," he said at last. "That way you'd know for sure, and so would he."

"That's what I thought. I couldn't understand why he didn't have me get tested in Nevada."

Russ wasn't about to tell her. Joe had seen her picture, noted the color of her hair and asked his attorney to arrange for her to fly to the island as soon as possible. When Russ's dad had argued for testing first, Joe refused. "I have this feeling she's Isabel's girl, Lou," Joe had insisted. "I want to see her. We'll do the damn tests while she's here."

No one could have predicted Joe would wind up being airlifted to Columbia Presbyterian Hospital at the same time Mari was flying to the island. So what was she? A truth-teller or a clever impostor?

"It would have been easier for everyone if the tests had been done in Nevada," Russ said, thinking not only of Joe and Mari, but of himself, as well. Negative tests would have exposed her, and his father would never have enlisted him as a spy. If they'd proved positive, then he wouldn't be in this unenviable position, either.

"That's what I meant," she said. "It's the not knowing that's so hard for me. And for Mr. Haskell as well, especially since he's ill. Is he my grandfather? I've never had one, you know."

A grandfather as wealthy as Joe Haskell was a real prize, Russ thought cynically, discounting her wistful tone. Denise had been quite the actress, but Mari was even better at it.

Waiting for Russ to say something, while looking at his withdrawn expression, Mari felt close to tears. Just as she feared, his attitude toward her had changed since she'd told him why she was on the island. She'd desperately needed a friend to confide in, and who else did she have here? Now everything was changed. She should have realized he might suspect she'd come under false pretenses—after all, his father was Mr. Haskell's best friend. And his attorney.

Without saying anything more, she rose and picked up the picnic basket. Russ stared at her for a moment before jumping up. As he folded the blanket, he said, "You're right, it's time for the next revelation."

"Oh, do you have one, too?" Despite trying to keep her voice even, she felt it quaver.

He gave her an odd look, one she couldn't quite decipher. A mixture of surprise and guilt? Surely not.

"An island revelation is what I meant," he said after a few seconds. "The next part of our tour is by water."

"You don't have to—"

He dropped the blanket and caught her by the shoulders. "I don't care why you came to Mackinac. You're here, that's what matters. Didn't we make that clear night before last?" His voice was strained, almost desperate.

Confused, she gazed up at him, into his green eyes, seeing a hunger that wiped everything from her mind but her own answering need. When he caught her to him, his mouth coming down hard on hers, she let go of the basket to hold him closer, responding eagerly to the wild passion in his kiss.

Nothing mattered to Russ but having Mari in his arms. Whatever she was, he wanted her with an intensity that couldn't be denied. Never mind his father, never mind Joe; nothing else mattered. He couldn't ever recall feeling like this and he didn't care. Kissing her wasn't enough; he needed more, needed everything.

Cupping her breast through the T-shirt she wore drove him higher. They should be naked, the two of them, making love in this meadow here and now. He could tell by her soft moans and by the way she clung to him that the same fiery urgency fueled her. He pulled away slightly to locate the blanket and, as he did, he heard voices.

"Damn tourists!" he blurted. Were there no secret places left on the island?

Releasing Mari, he did his best to cool down, picking up the blanket again.

She gave him an impish grin. "Remember, you make your living from those poor tourists."

Never mind how unruffled and collected she looked, the husky tone of her voice revealed how much she'd been aroused. By him. For him. He grinned at her. The day was far from over. He even managed a friendly hello when two couples emerged into the clearing.

By the time he and Mari had driven back to town, dropped the horse and buggy at the stables and walked down to the marina where his sailboat waited, Russ had filed her confession away for later evaluation. This wasn't his father's or Joe's day, this was his. His and Mari's.

"So this is the revelation you meant," she said as she helped him ready the boat.

He didn't care to be reminded of revelations at the moment, so he began quizzing her about how a desert gal knew her way around a sailboat.

"Lake Tahoe is less than an hour away from the ranch," she told him. "Plus there's Topaz Lake to the east and Washoe to the north. I'll have you know I also fish."

What he'd intended to do was circumnavigate the island, pointing out various sites, but that was before he'd kissed her in the meadow. All he really wanted now was to find a secluded spot to anchor and finish what they'd begun. Unlikely during tourist season here, but there were other islands nearby. A quick look through binoculars at Bois Blanc Island showed him a number of boats anchored there, and it was the same at Round Island.

The moment might have to be postponed, but he sure as hell wasn't giving it up.

"Would you like a view of the Haskell house from the water?" he asked. "It and the other old Victorian cottages along the West Bluff?"

She nodded, asking, "Is your father's place one of them?"

"His is on the East Bluff, also Victorian, but smaller."

"Is your mother still alive?"

He shook his head. "She died five years ago." It'd been his quiet, sweet-tempered mother who'd asked him if he were sure he wanted to marry Denise. He'd realized later—too late—that it had been as much of a warning as she was capable of giving.

"Do you have any brothers or sisters?"

"My sister Amy is five years younger. She's a psychologist living in California." Amy hadn't underplayed her warning to Russ before his wedding.

"Skip town right now, Russ," she'd advised. "You'll be sorry if you don't."

He'd laughed, pretending to think she meant marriage in general, not Denise specifically.

Before he realized what he was doing, Russ found himself saying, "Neither my mother nor Amy thought Denise and I were well suited, but I didn't listen."

"How about your father?"

"He was for the marriage." As he spoke, Russ realized this wasn't quite true. "He didn't express any opinion," he amended.

"Willa thinks you might not be poisonous," Mari told him.

He raised an eyebrow.

"She raises rattlers for their venom and can tell a harmless snake from the poisonous kind with one good look. She rates men the same way."

"I'm harmless?"

"No man is. Actually, even so-called harmless snakes often bite people who handle them. But the bites aren't fatal."

"So this isn't a fatal attraction we have going here?"

Mari's smile faded, but she spoke lightly enough. "As Willa would say, could be it's too soon to tell."

When they rounded the island so the West Bluff could be seen, he pointed out the Haskell house. "You can tell it by the single cupola."

"With the telescope in it."

"I wonder if it still is?"

"I haven't been up to look." After a moment, Mari added, "You know, Diana thinks Mr. Haskell banished a portrait of Isabel to the attic. Pauline says that isn't true, because she inventories the attic every spring. It just occurred to me there's a possibility that portrait might be in the cupola. What do you think?"

"It's important to you to find this picture?"

"Yes. All the family photos of Isabel have been destroyed, apparently, so I don't know what she looked like. I really would like to know. In case…" Her voice trailed off.

He knew why, but he wasn't going to go there right now. Especially since she'd just given him such a great idea.

"We could explore the cupola together," he

said. "I'll see if the telescope's still there and you can search for the portrait."

Her face lit up. "Oh, would you come with me?"

"Why not? We'll zip back to the marina and take a look right now." His motives were so ulterior he almost felt guilty, but he figured she must at least guess what he had in mind, nonfatal attraction or not.

Chapter Six

When Russ and Mari entered the Haskell house, neither Pauline nor Diana were anywhere in sight. Mari set the picnic basket down on the entry table and led the way upstairs, pausing by the door she knew led up to the cupola. As before, it was unlocked, and Russ opened it.

"When I was a kid," he said, as they started up the steps, "I couldn't decide which I liked the best—the spiral stairs or the telescope."

"I do believe this is the first spiral staircase I've ever climbed," she said, wondering how it would have been to be a child spending summers in this house with loving parents.

Not that Blanche and Stan hadn't been loving parents who'd given her a happy childhood in Nevada. Mari had no complaints. Still, ever since her uncle had told her the truth about her parentage, she'd felt a nagging need to learn more about her birth parents. She was on this island to discover whether her mother really was Isabel Haskell, but how about her father? His name on the original birth certificate had been listed as Elias Grant. As far as Mari knew, he'd never been told he had a daughter.

Would he care? Or was he like Danny Boy, who'd left a woman and the child he'd fathered back in California, to come to Nevada and find someone new to romance. Mari had no clue to what her father might or might not have done, but she'd never forget the day she'd found out that Danny Boy had skipped out on his responsibilities and she had confronted him about it.

"That's *her* problem," he'd said of the woman he'd deserted. "She might have been living with me, but for all I know the kid could be some other guy's."

What a hockey puck! Mari had dropped him— fast. It still upset her to think she'd ever been attracted to a guy who had no heart, much less a conscience. Now here she was, trusting another man. Not too smart, was it? Russ had given her a reason for his divorce, but she hadn't heard his ex-wife's side of it, had she?

"You've made it to the top, you know," Russ said, bringing her back to the present. How long had she been standing at the head of the spiral staircase, lost in the past?

"I was thinking about the man listed as my father—Elias Grant," she told him. "Will I ever know if he's dead or alive?"

Russ well knew that as soon as Joe had received the letter from Mari's uncle, Russ's father had hired private investigators to search for Elias Grant. So far, he hadn't been found.

"It's so strange to discover my mother was a person Aunt Blanche didn't even know. According to my uncle, Blanche never found out where my mother came from, other than 'off the bus.'"

For some reason Russ didn't doubt this part of Mari's story. How could he, when he could see the sad and lost expression on her face? Was there any possibility that she and her uncle could be telling the truth? Not that it would ensure she was Isabel Haskell's child, even if they were. The very vagueness of Mari's background may have been what had prompted them to have her pose as the Haskell heir.

"The red telescope," he said, turning from her as well as his thoughts. "There it is, like I remember."

She cleared her throat. "Oh, yes, I see the telescope."

"Everything's the same—the paneled walls, the red velvet chaise longue, the rosewood secretary, the rug—everything."

Mari took a few steps into the round room. "What a wonderful place—no wonder you liked to be up here. The view is spectacular."

"Let me focus the finderscope on the harbor."

"Didn't the old sea captains have telescopes on their ships? Oh, no, I'm wrong. They had spyglasses."

Spyglasses. The word jolted him. The spy with the spyglass? No, dammit, this was a telescope. But what was he? To rid himself of the uncomfortable thought, Russ said the first thing that came to mind. "They're not ships on the Great Lakes, they're boats, even the big ones. At least until the seagoing cargo ships began coming through the St. Lawrence Seaway. But lake captains still command boats, not ships."

She raised her eyebrows. "I stand corrected."

His smile was apologetic. "Didn't mean to lecture." He fiddled with the scope finder until the harbor came clearly into view. "Come look."

She obeyed, standing so close to him that her faint scent of lilacs surrounded him in an erotic web. "Mari," he murmured.

When she lifted her head from the eyepiece to turn to him, he gazed into her tawny eyes and was lost. He saw her pupils dilate as he bent to kiss her, then his lips met hers, she was in his arms and nothing else mattered.

His hands slid up under her T-shirt, finding and releasing her bra closure, freeing her breasts to his touch. Perfect beasts, designed to drive a man out of his mind with desire. Not that his mind was functioning, anyway. Not with her softness pressing against him, conjuring up an image of her naked, lying against the red velvet of the chaise.

Mari, feeling that she was melting, that her knees might give way at any moment, sighed in anticipation when he lifted her into his arms.

A moment later he sat her on the chaise, immediately lifting her shirt over her head and sliding off her bra. He eased down beside her, turning her toward him to run his tongue over each nipple in turn before taking one breast into his mouth. Pleasurable shivers coursed along her nerves, warmth pooling deep within. By the time he moved his caresses to her other breast she'd lost all sense of time or place. Nothing existed except Russ.

He eased her down until she was lying on the chaise, then he knelt on the rug and took off her shoes and socks. Unzipping her jeans, he slid them down her legs, along with her panties. He leaned over and ran his tongue along her abdomen, lower and lower until he reached the inside of her thighs. She quivered with escalating need, reaching a crescendo when he came to her heated center.

She wanted, she needed. "Russ," she moaned. "Oh, Russ."

And then—miraculously, it seemed—he, too, was naked and rising over her, filling her with his hardness, his rhythmic thrusts taking her with him to somewhere she'd never been before, a place she never wanted to leave.

Still holding her, in the warmth of the afterglow, Russ made the mistake of trying to ease onto his side. There was no room and they both rolled off the low chaise onto the rug. She looked at him and began to giggle. He chuckled, lightheaded with happiness and wishing he'd never have to let her go. Reaching up, he grabbed the afghan from the arm of the chaise and pulled it over them.

"I'm just a romantic at heart," he told her.

"You're admitting you have one?"

"A heart? Don't we all?"

"No. Not everyone." She bent her head until her ear lay on his left chest. "There's something beating in there," she murmured. "I hope it's a heart."

He gave her a squeeze. "I always thought it was." He slid his hand along her side until he reached her left breast. Just under it he could feel the steady thump of her own heart, but at the moment, he was more interested in other things. Cupping her breast, he ran his thumb over her nipple.

"I don't think that's my heart," she said.

Sliding his hand over to fondle her other breast, he said, "I already know you have one heart."

He eased his hand downward. "There's another place I need to investigate, though."

As he reached her warm and moist center, her hand closed over his rapidly stiffening arousal. He gave an involuntary sound of pleasure. By the time she urged him onto his back, he was extremely ready.

"Wait," he said, groping for his discarded jeans.

After he managed to extract what he needed, she slid it onto him, driving him wild with her touch. He thought he'd die from anticipation before she fitted herself over him and they again entered into the age-old dance of mating.

Making love with her was so different, like nothing he'd ever experienced. Once they'd reached the peak again and she collapsed onto him, he still wasn't ready to let her go.

"We can't stay like this for the rest of the day," she murmured at last.

"Why not?"

"For one thing, Pauline might come looking."

Russ released Mari reluctantly.

After they were dressed and the afghan once again draped sedately over the arm of the chaise longue, she said, "Are you sure the only reason you wanted to come here was to check on the telescope?"

Noting the impish glint in her eye, he nodded. "How was I to know I'd wind up being seduced?"

"I was under the impression that you seduced me."

"Can we agree on mutual seduction? Not that I haven't had it in mind since I got my first view of that enticing butt of yours on the fence in Nevada.''

She rolled her eyes. "Men." Then she looked carefully around the small room. "At least you found the telescope. I don't see any place a portrait could be hidden up here."

A mental picture flashed before Russ, something he'd known as a kid he wasn't supposed to see. He'd been coming up the spiral staircase in his bare feet because his shoes and socks were muddy and the housekeeper before Pauline had made him take them off before she'd let him in the house. So Joe, up in the cupola, hadn't heard him. Ten-year-old Russ had almost been to the top and ready to call out, when he saw Joe slide back a panel in the wall, put a large oblong object inside and close the panel.

A secret panel, Russ had told himself. Joe'll be mad if he knows I saw. So he had eased back halfway down the stairs and begun to whistle as he started up again. He'd been tempted to look for the panel a few times when he was alone in the room, but he never had. And then he'd forgotten about it until this moment.

"There is a place," he told Mari.

Russ tried three panels before he found the right one. Inside was what looked like the large oblong object he'd seen Joe put there so many years ago. It was wrapped in a soft cloth and, as he lifted it free, he could feel what was under the material. A canvas on a stretch frame.

He handed it to Mari, explaining how he knew about the secret panel. "At the time I had no idea it was a portrait," he finished.

By then she was sitting on the floor, carefully unwrapping the canvas.

He stared down at what she'd uncovered—an oil portrait of an adolescent girl. A girl with the same color hair as Mari's. But Isabel, if that's who it was, had blue not sherry-colored eyes, and instead of Mari's rounder face, she had a pointed chin.

For a long time Mari didn't take her gaze from the portrait. Finally she looked up at him and said in a flat tone, "I don't look like Isabel, do I?"

"If it is Isabel," he equivocated.

"We both know it must be. Why else would he hide it?"

"Your hair's the same color." He knew perfectly well hair could be dyed any color—in fact, his father had mentioned that to him before he left for Nevada. Still, if Mari and her uncle had never seen a colored photo of Isabel—and how could they, when the media hadn't been able to uncover any?—it'd be tricky to get even close to this unusual shade.

"But we don't look anything alike."

He almost told her she might resemble her father before he realized what he was about to do. Here he was supposed to be uncovering her as a scam artist. Why would he want to convince her she could be Isabel's daughter? Damn, she'd almost converted him into a believer, and that'd never do. "You're prettier," he said, aware that wasn't what she wanted to hear.

Mari stared into Russ's green eyes, wondering what he was thinking. Was he telling her the truth about forgetting the secret panel, or had he known all along Isabel's portrait was hidden behind it? She mentioned looking for a portrait before they'd ever climbed up here, yet, he hadn't said a word about the panel until now. Hadn't she learned better than to trust any man?

But he wasn't any man, he was Russ. They'd just made love together, the most wonderful experience of her entire life.

Suddenly he jerked her to her feet and wrapped his arms about her. "Don't look so woebegone," he ordered.

Without warning, she burst into tears.

He patted her back, murmuring soothing words

she didn't try to interpret. More than words, she needed the comfort of his arms. Wrapped in them, she felt safe. Whatever happened, she could count on Russ. He must care about her or he wouldn't be so concerned about her feelings.

Later, when she'd stopped crying and mopped her wet face, she tried to explain. "I was so sure that, if I could find a picture of Isabel, I'd know one way or the other if I could be her daughter. But I still don't."

"The DNA and blood tests should be conclusive."

She sighed. "I guess so." She took a long look at the portrait. "Poor Isabel, to wind up alone and sick in a strange city. How could that have happened? Where was my father?" Her voice rose. "I don't want a Danny Boy for a father."

Russ touched her shoulder. "You're not making much sense."

"None of it makes any sense." Aware that tears threatened again, she took a deep breath, struggling to calm herself.

After Russ rewrapped the portrait and replaced it behind the panel, he gently urged her toward the staircase, saying, "Let's go down and see what Diana's up to. You could use a cup of coffee, and I thought I smelled her famous strawberry-rhubarb pie when we first entered the house.''

Composing herself, Mari said, ''So it's true—the way to a man's heart really is through his stomach.''

''I'm out of luck. She's already married.''

''Too bad.'' Mari smiled at him. What a great guy he was. And more. Much more than she was ready to deal with right now.

''Speaking of food, how about lunch tomorrow?'' he said. ''I'll come by about noon.''

Should she say no? She'd been so overwhelmed by what had happened in the cupola that maybe she should draw back and take some time to think things over. Hadn't Willa warned her she needed to wait awhile before jumping into another relationship? On the other hand, what Mari really wanted was to be with Russ. After thinking things over, she might well come up with the same conclusion—that she wanted to be with Russ, no matter what.

''Sounds good to me,'' she told him.

Chapter Seven

The next morning Mari woke up with the feeling that the day ahead of her would be wonderful. Her lunch date with Russ wasn't until twelve, so the morning was hers. She needed to think of something to do other than spending it looking forward to seeing him. She'd been to the fort and Russ had shown her other island sites of interest. Maybe she'd ask Pauline for a suggestion of where to go.

"Let's see," Pauline said, when the question had been posed. "How about the Crack in the Island? Have you been there?"

Mari shook her head. "It sounds interesting. Tell me about the crack."

"I can tell you how to get there." Pauline proceeded to do so. "If you like legends, go find Diana and ask her what the ancient Indians used to believe about the crack. She knows all those old tales."

Diana was happy to oblige over coffee and a cinnamon roll. "The Land of the Turtle—that's Mackinac Island—once had giants living here. When the Great Spirit of the Chippewa ordered them off the earth, he changed some into rocks, calling them waiting spirits. The bad ones, though, became men with no hearts, cruel and evil, and he called them wandering demons. One of the giants refused to become either a rock or a bad man, so he tried to escape to the Land Below, where the dead dwell. Long ago the Great Spirit had stamped his foot and made this deep bottomless crack that the giant tried to climb down, but the weather was cold and his fingers froze to the mouth of the opening. The Great Spirit decreed he must hang within the crack forever as punishment.

"If you go there you have to be careful not to step on the giant's fingers or misfortune will follow," Diana added.

"Thanks for the warning."

"I heard tell some geologists think the crack came during an ages-ago earthquake," Diana added. "You know how those scientists are, though—others think underground waters eroded the soft rock away, forming a fissure. There really was an underground lake there, way back when everyone says."

"So I have a choice of the Great Spirit, an earthquake or erosion," Mari joked. "Whichever I choose, though, I'll be careful not to step on the giant's frozen fingers."

She set off, finding with little difficulty the woodland path that Pauline had told her of, and enjoying the walk, with the trees on either side thrusting out their new green leaves of spring. Since she'd seen cracks in California left by earthquakes, Mari didn't expect to be impressed, but when she came to the deep, jagged fissure running through the stone, she gazed in awe. Peering cautiously down into the darkness, she could see no bottom. Awesome. No wonder the Native Americans had their own version of its creation.

As she stepped back, her foot struck a rock fragment, making her stumble sideways until she regained her balance. She glanced around to see what she'd stumbled over, then chided herself.

There was no such thing as a giant's frozen fingers. How could she possibly think of misfortune when Russ would be calling for her at noon?

Walking back along the path, with birds chirping around her, she relived their moments in the cupola, becoming so lost in reverie that she was startled when she rounded a bend and encountered several women walking toward her. She returned their greetings and went on, glancing at her watch.

Before she reached the end of the path, she saw someone else coming her way. A man. Russ! Her breath caught and her heart jolted in her chest. It was all she could do not to run to him.

When he reached her, he held out his arms and she all but fell into them, hungry for his kiss. When they finally came up for air, she asked, "How did you know where I was?"

"Got to the house early and Diana told me you were out here braving the frozen giant."

"I just hope I didn't step on one of his fingers."

"Don't even think it. Misfortune has no place on this island."

He let her go, capturing her hand in his as they started back the way he'd come, his own words ringing in his ears. What a stupid thing to say, considering the circumstances that had brought her here, and his own entanglement in the situation.

With an effort of will he brushed it all aside. He was with Mari. They'd be together for hours. Nothing else was important.

"Since I last talked to you," he said, "we've been invited to lunch on a friend's yacht. How about it?"

"Surely I wasn't invited."

"Surely you were. He told me to bring a friend. Aren't we friends?"

"A jeans and T-shirt lunch?"

"That's what I'm wearing—why not you?" He peered down at her. "Especially considering what you do for jeans and a T-shirt." His fingertips brushed lightly over her breast, making heat pool in his loins.

"Shouldn't have done that," he said ruefully, "since there's no place around here to take it any further."

She gave him a saucy smile. "What makes you think I'd be interested?"

"Oh, just a hunch." He couldn't resist rubbing a thumb over her erect nipple to prove his point, even though it aroused him even more.

Mari was going to be hard to forget if the state he was in from barely touching her was any indication. He'd have to give up a twosome at lunch to take her aboard the yacht, but maybe it was just as well. He could use some cooling down time.

"So it's a go?" he asked.

She shrugged. "Lunch is lunch."

"He's an old law school buddy. He's not staying on the island, just stopped by for a few days, living on the yacht."

She smiled at Russ, but said nothing more. He swung their joined hands as they walked, enjoying the contact. Finally they came out on the road.

"You up to walking to the marina?" he asked.

"No problem."

"If a carriage comes by with space for us we can always hitch a ride."

"Is your friend married?" she asked after a while.

"Roger?" He hesitated. "He introduced the woman with him as Adrienne. To tell the truth I can't remember if that was his wife's name or not, so he could be divorced. Or even married again, who knows?"

"She's his girlfriend," Mari said.

"Why?"

"I think Roger would have said something like, 'You remember my wife, Adrienne,' if she was his first wife. If she was his second wife, he would have said, 'This is my wife, Adrienne.' But he just gave her name, so the odds are I'm right. Not that it makes any difference.''

Russ grinned at her. ''So when I introduce you simply as Mari, I'll have given myself away as having a gorgeous girlfriend.''

''Roger must have known you were married at one time.''

''He did. But he may not have heard about the divorce.'' He shot her a mischievous look. ''Maybe I can confuse him by saying, 'You remember my wife, Mari.''

She tried not to show her reaction. Though she knew he was teasing, she found herself upset.

Apparently she didn't hide her reaction well enough, because he said, ''You don't care for that idea?''

Answering honestly, Mari said, ''No, not really.'' She couldn't be sure why. Joking wasn't lying; it wasn't that. Maybe it had to do with her not wanting to be confused, even for a moment, with Denise. Which was silly.

When they reached the marina and Russ pointed out Roger's boat to Mari, she said, ''Whoa. That really is a yacht.''

''Forty-footer.''

"I've never been aboard a yacht," she confessed, telling herself she wasn't intimidated. If she actually was a Haskell, she supposed she'd have to grow accustomed to evidences of wealth like this luxurious craft. For some reason, the thought disturbed her.

Russ hailed Roger. "Permission to board," he called.

A red-haired man rose up from a lounge chair. "Russ. Didn't see you coming. Climb aboard, by all means."

The blonde reclining in the chair next to him stayed where she was as they came on deck. Even when Roger said, "Adrienne, our guests are here," all she did was wave a languid hand.

When Russ introduced Mari simply by her first name, Adrienne sat up and looked her over. Apparently being identified as a girlfriend rather than a wife made Mari more worthy of notice.

"So glad you could make it," Adrienne drawled.

"What would you like to drink?" Roger asked.

Russ had a beer and Mari settled for orange soda, while the other two chose white wine.

Soon Roger took Russ off to show him around the boat, leaving the two women alone. "Do you come to Mackinac Island often?" Mari asked.

"My first time," Adrienne admitted, sipping at her wine. "Quaint places aren't really my thing." Again she looked searchingly at Mari. "Did Roger say Russ's last name was Simon?"

Mari nodded.

"Bull's-eye," Adrienne said with a satisfied smile. "I thought I recognized the name. A friend of mine was married to him for a while."

Before she could curb her tongue, Mari blurted, "Denise?"

"Do you know her?"

"No, not at all."

"I didn't meet Denise till after the divorce. She and I see eye to eye about priorities."

Mari bit back the questions she longed to ask. What did Denise look like and what was her version of the breakup? Also, just what were those priorities?

Deciding she could ask the last, Mari murmured, "Priorities?"

Adrienne finished her wine and set the glass on a table near her chair. "You know, like what's important in life and what's not really. Take money. Without enough of it, life sucks."

Ever since Mari had been old enough to understand, she'd known the Crowleys had to watch their spending very carefully. Things had improved after Uncle Stan had quit gambling, but there'd never been money to spare. Yet she'd had a happy childhood, and Blanche and Stan had always seemed content.

Aware that Adrienne was waiting for a reply, Mari said the only thing that came to mind. "Like living in poverty."

Adrienne frowned. "Well, that, too. But what I meant was, where can you go, what's there to do, if there's not enough money? You can't even buy decent clothes."

Eyeing her hostess's designer outfit, Mari managed a polite smile, since she could think of nothing tactful to say. Were these Denise's priorities, too, as Adrienne had implied?

"Wait until I tell Denise that Russ has acquired a girlfriend with hair to die for," Adrienne said. "Do tell me what your hairdresser mixes together to get that amazing color."

It wasn't the first time Mari had fielded that question. "I was born with it." Nor was it the first time her answer earned a disbelieving look.

"Marriage is for the birds, as far as I'm concerned," Adrienne continued. "If you're unattached, you can just move on without any messy legalities when you get bored."

Mari wasn't sure she subscribed to this philosophy. On the other hand she hadn't yet met a man she cared to marry. Russ? She shook her head, telling herself firmly it was too early in their relationship to be sure one way or the other.

The men returned and lunch was served. The meal passed pleasantly enough, even though Mari had realized early on that she and Adrienne had little in common.

Later, after they'd thanked their host and left his boat—*The Tort-Us,* Mari noted—Russ led the way up the hill toward the fort.

"There's a good spot to overlook the harbor up there," he told her. "It was great to see Roger again. You were right about Adrienne—they're not married."

"She knows Denise," Mari said.

Russ slanted her a look, raising his eyebrow.

Mari shrugged. "She just mentioned the fact."

After that he was silent until they reached the lookout, where they leaned on the stone barrier and gazed down at the village and the harbor. Beyond was the lake with the ferries coming and going between Upper and Lower Michigan.

"I don't think about Denise much anymore," Russ said at last. "We should never have married. I admit the experience has soured me on that particular institution."

"Adrienne said she didn't believe in it."

"How about you?"

"I'm not sure. If I meet anyone who makes me think I'd like to try it, I'll let you know."

"You do that," he said, smiling at her as he took her hand and turned them away from the view.

"Mind if we take a look at my horses?" he asked. "I like to check on the ones at rest every day when I'm on the island."

"Then you don't spend the entire summer on the island?"

"I shuttle between here and my horse farm downstate. Lucky I happened to be on the island when you arrived."

Lucky, yes. A coincidence? But coincidences did happen. Mari pushed the thought from her mind and said, "You know me and horses. Let's go."

On the way to the stables he explained how horses were rotated for carriage duty, so there were always fresh ones available. "They get more rest than the drivers," he finished.

Once satisfied his Blues were in good shape, Russ tried to think of a place to take Mari where they'd be alone. They couldn't chance the cupola again—Pauline was no fool, and he didn't want to place Mari in an awkward position. For some reason he balked at bringing her to his dad's cottage, maybe because he knew damn well he shouldn't be feeling this way about Mari. Making love to her sure as hell wasn't what his father had asked him to do.

It's what he wanted to do, though. Urgently.

"Up for a buggy ride?" he asked.

"Why not?"

He took the road through the woods, an arm around her as he let the horse amble along.

"The island is so different from anywhere else. Right now we might be the only two on it," she commented.

"Until the next batch of tourists comes along. But I know the feeling. And speaking of feelings…" He let his words trail off as he guided the horse onto an overgrown trail and halted him at a right angle to the road, so the buggy back and sides would offer some concealment.

Easing closer to Mari, he pulled her into his arms and kissed her. He felt her immediate, eager response down to his toenails. Forgetting everything else, he savored her taste and her softness pressing against him. Nothing else mattered.

Mari realized she'd been waiting for this moment ever since she'd opened her eyes that morning—to be alone with Russ in a secluded place so they could kiss and hold each other without interruption. How she'd gotten herself in such a state she didn't quite understand, but at the moment she didn't care. He tasted of the mint frappé they'd been served for dessert at lunch, and of himself. He tasted like Russ, the most addictive flavor she could imagine.

He slid his hand under her shirt, pushing up her bra until he cupped a breast. Need gripped her, heating her, making her cling to him. She moaned in pleasure as he dipped his head to replace his hand with his mouth.

When he finally lifted his head and looked at her, she couldn't speak.

"You're driving me wild," he said hoarsely, "and this is no place for what I have in mind."

"No, it's not," she agreed, a pinch of sense returning to her.

He let her go and she rearranged her clothes, her body tingling with need.

After a few moments, he urged the horse back onto the road again. "I hope you realize I don't want to take you home," he said. "But since I can't have what I want, I'm going to do just that."

Neither did she want him to take her home and leave her.

"I have a dinner meeting on the mainland this evening with the owners of the carriage company I lease my horses to, so I can't see you until morning. Breakfast at our usual café around eight?"

"Yes," she said, her voice still sounding breathless.

He sighed. "It's going to be a long night."

Chapter Eight

Back at home after the meeting, Russ couldn't sleep. Tired of tossing and turning, he rose and padded out to the enclosed back porch, where he stared up at the nearly full moon shining through the tall pines his grandfather had planted as a young man. Grandpa Ed had been an honorable man. Russ's father was, too. Why, then, had he asked Russ to vet Marigold Crowley?

Spying might be an old profession and even a necessary one, but, as applied to himself, Russ couldn't think of it as honorable. The only possible good that could come from this was a healing of the breach between himself and his dad, which was why he'd agreed to do such a thing in the first place. Maybe he was right in thinking that was why his father had asked for the favor, as a way of letting Russ know he was ready to let bygones be bygones. It was certainly the only reason he'd agreed to do it.

Mari was meeting him for breakfast in the morning. How he wished she were in his bed here and now. They could snuggle together after their lovemaking and he'd tell her—what? That he was a plant, a mole from the enemy camp, sent to spy out her scheme and thwart it? He grimaced.

Despite himself, he was beginning to believe in the possibility that she might be Joe's granddaughter. If that turned out to be true, then they'd be seeing a lot more of each other. Which was fine with him, except he could hardly expect her to be thrilled about ever seeing him again if she learned why he'd finagled an acquaintance with her. Even if she wasn't a Haskell.

Best not to tell her. It was only a lie of omission.

Great, not only a spy, but a liar, too.

Dammit, he wanted to go on seeing her. Making love in the cupola had done nothing to ease his need for her. Made it worse, as a matter of fact. They ought to be together right now. He leaned against a post, closing his eyes, remembering the softness of her skin, smoother than the velvet of the chaise....

Shaking his head, he opened the screen door and sat on the top step. The night air was cool, moonlight silvered the shrubs and the scent of lilacs from the beginning-to-bloom bushes wrapped him in the memory of Mari's scent, of how she fit into his arms, of the passionate response she brought to their mating.

Fine, now he was aroused as well as sleepless. The neighbor's yellow tomcat padded up the steps, rubbed his head against Russ's knees for a moment, then took off into the moonlit night.

"Hope you're luckier than I am," Russ muttered as he reentered the house, where he paced from room to room. He didn't want to believe in Mari, but he did. At least to the extent that she really did believe she might be Isabel's daughter. Whether she was or not remained to be proved, but he was convinced she had no part in a scam. What the hell, even her uncle might really believe she could be a Haskell, in which case there was no scam at all. Which was what Russ intended to tell his father when he called him in the morning.

But what, if anything, was he going to tell Mari?

His father's phone call woke him up at seven.

"Good news," Lou Simon said. "Joe's agreed to have the girl tested before he goes back to the island. He's doing well. Shouldn't be more than a few days before he's discharged. Of course, he'll still have to have the bypass when he's fully recovered from this episode."

"Glad to hear he's improving," Russ said, smothering a yawn.

"What about the girl?"

Russ told him his conclusions.

"Sure you're not smitten?" Lou demanded.

Smitten. What a word. "I like her," he admitted. "She comes across as honest. The point is she could be Isabel's daughter."

Lou snorted. "The DNA results'll take care of that in a hurry. Come on, Son, she's just another scam artist. The seventh one to date. I told Joe not to go on TV—knew it would attract impostors—but he's always been a stubborn so-and-so."

"I think you're wrong about Mari."

"To get you going she must be even prettier in

person than in that picture her uncle sent. Thought you swore off women.''

''Mari is different,'' Russ insisted. ''She might not be Joe's heir, but she definitely isn't a scam artist.'' Aware that he was getting riled, and not wanting to argue with his father, he changed the subject. ''Are you coming back with Joe?''

''He asked me to, so I'll stay on here until he's discharged, but I'll arrange for a lab technician to go to the island to get the blood and DNA samples right away.''

''Okay. See you soon.''

After hanging up, Russ took a quick shower and dressed, knowing he'd have to break the news about the tests to Mari at breakfast.

Mari slept through most of the night, but woke from a bad dream when it was getting light. In her dream, she thought she'd been with Russ, but then he turned his back to her. When he faced her again, it wasn't him at all, but a stranger with green eyes who told her to go home, she wasn't wanted here.

She sat up in bed, hugging herself. True, when she'd arrived on Mackinac, she hadn't felt she belonged on the island or in this house. But gradually that had changed. Now the house seemed familiar. Pauline and Diana were friendly, and Russ...

She sighed. Somehow her perspective had shifted until, though she still wished to learn about her parents, Russ and what he thought of her meant more to her than anything else. She hadn't planned for that to happen, but somehow it had.

Shaking her head as though to dispel the shards of the dream as well as her thoughts, she rose and began to ready herself for the new day. With Russ.

Later, as she walked down the hill to the café where they were to meet for breakfast, she found herself hurrying faster and faster, impatient to be with him again.

He was outside the restaurant waiting for her, and immediately ushered her through the door, leaving her a bit disappointed. While she hadn't expected a passionate embrace on the busy main street of the village, she'd anticipated at least a quick hug. He'd hardly smiled.

After they were seated, she decided he looked troubled. "Is something wrong?" she asked.

Instead of answering, he said, "Do you think your uncle might remember more of what happened the day your aunt found Ida Grant in the casino rest room? Where the bus she got off came from, for example?''

Somewhat taken aback, Mari said, ''I don't know.''

''It might give us a clue to where your father was at the time.'' He frowned. ''What did you mean yesterday when you said you didn't want a 'Danny Boy' father?''

The waitress brought coffee, a welcome respite for Mari. No way did she want to tell him about Danny Boy.

She watched Russ take a swallow of coffee and then look at her with raised eyebrows.

''Well, if you know the words to the song,'' she said resignedly, ''you know Danny Boy went away and didn't come back.''

''That's all you meant?''

To her distress, she blushed, something she often did when she tried to be evasive.

''So there is more.''

''Not much,'' she snapped, irked at his persistence. ''I went with a guy named Danny for a while, till I found out he'd deserted a woman and child in another state. Not only did I lose all respect for him, but I can't stand to be lied to. That's when the song came to mind. Now I can't help wondering why Elias Grant wasn't there for Ida.''

Russ glanced down at the menu. "What're you having?" he asked.

She stared at him. He had no comment, after he'd dragged the information out of her? What was the matter with him?

"Buttermilk pancakes," she muttered.

Breakfast was not a tremendous success, even though the food was delicious. As they sipped a second cup of coffee while waiting for the check, Russ set his cup down so hard the coffee splashed onto the table.

"My father called this morning," he said. "Someone will be coming in the next day or so to take a blood and DNA sample from you."

"Oh." She thought about it and added, "It'll be a relief to get that over with." Thinking some more, she said, "Did you think you were the bearer of bad news? Is that why you're so glum?

His smile was wry. "In the old days they used to shoot the bearer of bad news."

"I never learned to shoot a gun, so you're safe. And, anyway, it's really good news. I'll soon find out one way or the other and stop lingering in limbo."

After they left the café, he took her hand and

she smiled at him, happy to think that what had bothered him was nothing for her to be upset about.

"Since our sail yesterday got sidetracked," he said, "I thought we'd try the boat again." He slanted a look at her. "Best reason I ever had for turning back to harbor."

"Uh, yes, it was pretty good."

"Pretty good?"

"Well, actually, indescribable."

"I can accept that." He began swinging her hand as they walked, and her heart lifted with her spirits.

In the marina she noticed the name of his boat again, and this time it registered. *"Evening Star,"* she said. "I just realized you must have named her after that old legend you told to me about the Sky People. You *are* a romantic."

He grinned at her. "Don't say I didn't warn you."

But his own words reminded him of what he still hadn't told her, and his grin faded. He didn't want to make the confession and, since the sailboat wouldn't be the best place for it anyway, he decided to put it off for the time being.

"So we're going to sail all around the island today?" Mari asked as they cleared the harbor.

Russ, troubled by his own thoughts, nodded. Since the wind was in a different direction than the day before, he opted to go round the opposite way. The sun was shining through thin clouds, too thin to hint of rain.

"This is the coolest the weather's been since I got here," she said. "You know what, though?"

He shook his head. "What?"

"The lilacs are finally starting to bloom. I was beginning to wonder if they ever would."

"Sooner or later, they always do." Pulling himself out of his unwelcome reverie, he began to point out sites of interest along the island's coastline.

They'd rounded the far end when Mari cried, "Oh, look at the bridge—isn't that weird?"

She gestured, and Russ, who hadn't so much as glanced at the Mackinac Bridge until then, saw that both ends were shrouded in fog, so that it seemed to be a bridge from nowhere to nowhere. He could have appreciated the sight more if he hadn't also noticed the grayness spreading toward them. At the same time the deep-throated, warning moans of the foghorns began sounding.

If they got caught in fog, he wouldn't be able to get back into the harbor until it cleared. The breeze was carrying them along at a decent clip, but they might not make it in time. It wasn't a big deal, so he decided to pick one of the tiny coves on this side of the island and anchor in it until the fog lifted.

"We may have to drop anchor and wait it out," he told Mari, belatedly noticing she was hugging herself. "Cold?" He reached out and drew her next to him.

As the fog reached gray tentacles toward the boat, he spotted one of the coves and tacked partway in, telling Mari what she could do to help. He dropped the sails and set the anchor just as grayness closed around them.

"The foghorns sound so mournful," she said. "I've never heard them before. Nevada does get fog, especially in the winter—a frost fog the Paiute call *pogonip*. It's not good for your lungs to be out in it . But we don't have foghorns."

"As long as we're anchored here close to shore, we're safe enough."

"I'm not worried, just a tad cold."

"We'll go down in the cabin where the blankets are," he said. "Watch your head."

The tiny cabin was so dark it might have been night outside. Holding Mari's hand, Russ was groping for the lantern with his free hand when she stumbled over something and fell against him.

He staggered into the bunk, involuntarily sprawling across it, Mari with him.

She began to chuckle. "I'd accuse you of planning this," she said, "except I can't figure out how you managed the fog."

"We romantics have our secret ways," he murmured as he shifted them both into a more comfortable position and then kissed her the way he'd been longing to do all morning.

Her enthusiastic response triggered a rush of need so acute he had trouble reining himself in. Holding Mari was like nothing else. She was like no other woman.

"Lilacs," he whispered into her ear. "You and lilacs." It didn't express the passion she evoked in him, passion mixed with a tenderness that surprised him, but those were the only words he could find.

His warm breath tickled Mari's ear, sending a series of tiny thrills along her nerves. She didn't understand what he meant, but that didn't matter because his whisper was part of their lovemaking. All that mattered was their being together, wrapped in each other's arms. She wanted him so much she trembled with need.

She could sense he was holding back, trying to restrain himself, but with her desire flaring like wildfire, restraint wasn't necessary. Sliding her hand down, she closed it around his arousal. He groaned, took her hand away and stripped off his clothes. By the time he finished undressing, she was naked, too, pressing against him, telling him with her body what she wanted.

When he thrust inside her she matched his rhythm, until he followed her over the crest. Holding each other, they coasted down, snuggling together under a blanket.

"Aunt Blanche had a word she used to describe the way you looked at breakfast," she said after a time. "Glum."

Russ ran a hand over her hip. "I'm cured."

"Was it only because you had to tell me about the tests? You were still pretty quiet until the fog caught us."

He cupped her breast. "Because I wanted to do this and couldn't."

"The truth?"

"Part of it, anyway." He lifted his head and kissed her, a long, slow kiss she felt clear down to the soles of her feet. If he was trying to convince her that actions spoke louder than words, he was certainly succeeding.

Their lovemaking the second time was slow and sensual, as she explored all the sensitive parts of his body while he caressed hers. Once they joined together, though, the journey to the top was wildly satisfying. He still held her afterward, his arms around her even after she could tell by his breathing that he'd drifted off to sleep. Content and drowsy, she closed her eyes.

Mari woke to find a ray of sunlight slanting in through the open hatch. She glanced at Russ and found him awake, looking at her. For a moment she thought his green eyes looked troubled, but then he smiled.

"First time I realized fog could be a sailor's friend," he said. Raising his head, he gave her a quick kiss and then slid off the bunk to start dressing.

Mari waited until he was on deck to retrieve her scattered clothes and get into them.

Their run back into the harbor was uneventful. "Lunch?" Russ asked as they disembarked in the marina.

"I don't know about you," she said, "but I plan to take a shower before I do anything else."

"Think Diana will feed me as well as you?" he said. "If so, we can shower together."

The thought of being naked in a shower with Russ made her knees weak, but it wouldn't be appropriate at the Haskell house. She slanted him a look.

"I take it that means no. Dinner tonight, then? You haven't been inside the Grand Hotel yet."

"I thought you said the Grand was for special occasions."

"Having dinner with you isn't special? Or don't you think having dinner with me is special?"

Mari made a face at him. "*Special* was your word, not mine. I'd enjoy going there." As she agreed, she silently thanked heaven she'd brought along the one dressy outfit.

After he dropped her off at the Haskell cottage, Mari met Pauline in the entry. "I won't be in for dinner this evening," she told he housekeeper. "Russ is taking me to the Grand Hotel."

Pauline smiled. "I've always thought of the Grand as the most romantic hotel in the country."

Mari sighed. *Romantic.* How like Russ.

That evening Russ arrived at the Haskell house in a surrey with a fringe on top, one with a driver—the island equivalent of a limo. Feeling like a teenager going to her first prom, Mari let Russ, who looked gorgeous in a red blazer, navy-blue tie and white slacks, escort her down the steps to the surrey.

"In my father's vernacular, you look smashing," he told her. "The lilac lady."

He was right about the color of her sleeveless silk shift with matching short jacket. The boutique clerk where she'd found it on sale in Reno had commented, "You're one of those rare gals who can wear this deep lilac shade. Lucky you, this is a terrific buy."

Under Russ's admiring gaze Mari did feel lucky. This promised to be a fabulous evening, maybe even the best of her entire life. She refused to wonder how many more evenings they'd spend together. As the Nevada Paiutes put it:

Yesterday is ashes.
Tomorrow is wood.
Only today can there be fire.

Chapter Nine

The interior of the Grand Hotel was every bit as impressive as its white-columned exterior. More impressive, actually, Mari thought, than any of Reno's big casinos, because the decor was restrained elegance, not gaudy sumptuousness.

"How long is that front porch, anyway?" she asked as they headed toward the dining room.

"A bit longer than two football fields."

She shook her head in amazement, noting that while diners in Nevada tended to wear mostly jeans, with the occasional black leather outfits of bikers, here there was no casual dress in the dining room, which added to the impression of elegance. They were shown to their table, where the waiter seated Mari. Shortly thereafter the wine waiter approached, and Russ discussed champagne with him, then ordered a bottle.

"Five courses?" Mari said to Russ once they were alone. "I'll never manage to get through them all. I wonder if the hotel was anything like this when it opened in 1887."

"Other than necessary restorations, I'd say not much is different. It's always been a showplace."

"Isabel must have come to the hotel sometimes. What do you suppose she thought of it?"

Russ shrugged. "Probably she took it for granted—the Grand was just part of the island."

"It's so sad she left and never came back to see her father."

"Joe took a long time to mellow."

Mari nodded. "Isabel must have been as stubborn as he was. Schisms within families tend to be hard to heal."

"I know." The words were out before he realized it. He met her inquiring glance with a wry smile. "My dad wasn't exactly enthusiastic when I decided to raise horses instead of going into his law firm. He more or less cut me off, like Joe did Isabel. If it hadn't been for a small inheritance that my grandmother had left me, I'm none too sure I'd have been successful.''

''You seem to be okay with him now, though.''

He could hardly tell her the truth. Taking a deep breath, he said, ''We're getting there.'' With relief he greeted the return of the wine waiter with the champagne. Why he and his father had reached a rapprochement was definitely not something he wished to discuss with Mari, especially not during dinner at the Grand Hotel.

Watching Mari's enthusiasm as she tasted each of the dishes set before her enhanced the meal for Russ.

Despite her prediction about not getting through five courses, she made a valiant try. Unlike Denise, she had no affectations and never appeared bored. Everything interested her. Luckily, even him.

What would happen if he told her why he'd come to Nevada? He closed his eyes momentarily, imagining her scorn. He'd misrepresented himself as truly as that Danny jerk she'd rejected, if in a different way.

By the time they left the hotel, his thoughts had grown so dark he had trouble keeping up an agreeable front.

''It's such a beautiful night,'' she said. ''Let's

walk. I can't believe these long twilights on the island. By now in Nevada, the sun is behind the Sierras and it's pitch-dark.''

"Do you miss your ranch?" he asked.

She sighed. "Sometimes a lot. I feel like I'm running in place here, accomplishing nothing. If it wasn't for you—" she smiled up at him, making him feel worse than ever—"I don't know if I could've stayed here this long."

Though he hadn't consciously planned to, he found their walk was taking them toward his father's cottage. Well, why not? When they reached it, he said, "This is where I'm staying. Want to sit on the porch for a while?"

She stopped to examine the house. "I never before realized how attractive Victorian architecture was."

"There are some horrible examples of it, too." He led her up the steps to the chairs on the front porch. She chose a wicker settee, but, restlessness gripping him, he lounged against one of the porch pillars instead.

The yellow tomcat from next door came over to greet them, jumping onto the settee beside Mari, who began petting him. "Yours?" she asked.

"He acts like he lives here, but he belongs to the neighbors."

"Listen to him purr—he's a sweetheart."

"You wouldn't say that if he woke you up at four in the morning caterwauling with other toms over the affections of a female."

She lifted her head, sniffing. "Do I smell lilacs?"

Welcoming the chance to move, he held out his hand to her, saying, "Backyard."

Skirting the house, he led her to where lilac bushes nestled around a small gazebo.

"What a glorious scent," she cried, dropping his hand to break off a bloom. "I love it. And the gazebo is charming." She climbed the two steps to the octagonal structure. "I have friends in Nevada who have a gazebo in the yard at their ranch. I've always wanted one."

He gazed at her standing in the dimness of twilight, dazed by the perfume of the lilacs and the beauty of Mari framed by the white gazebo. When she held her hands out to him, for an instant he couldn't move, then in a couple strides he mounted the steps and clasped her hands in his.

"My lilac lady," her murmured, gazing down at her, knowing he'd remember this moment all his life.

She smiled at him so trustingly that his heart turned over. She wasn't the impostor; in a different sense, he was, because he was pretending to be something he wasn't. Russ Simon wasn't what she thought he was—just a guy interested in her. Interested was putting it mildly, but the undercurrent of "is she or isn't she the missing heir" flowed continuously, even though he now believed her to be on the island honestly.

Gathering her to him, he covered her mouth with his, doing his best to put all he felt into the kiss.

The touch of Russ's lips was so gentle and loving that it almost brought tears to Mari's eyes. He seemed different tonight, but that wasn't necessarily bad. Maybe their relationship was changing, becoming as intimate emotionally as it was physically.

Love? The thought both intrigued and frightened her. She wasn't ready, was she?

He deepened the kiss and she flowed against him, intensely, passionately aware of his hard body pressing against her.

A raucous yowl startled them both into pulling apart. The yowl was followed by another, then such furious growling and hissing that Mari realized the arguing toms must be somewhere in the lilac bushes circling the gazebo.

"What'd I tell you?" Russ said. "Your 'sweetheart' is showing his other side, like most males do, sooner or later."

She wondered at the thread of bitterness in his voice.

Taking her arm, he led her, back around the house to the street, and they resumed walking, somewhat to her surprise. Was there some reason he hadn't invited her into the house?

It took a few minutes to orient herself as to where they were on the island, and when she did, she found they were headed in the direction of the Haskell house. So he was taking her home. Well, that was okay; she'd invite him inside.

"Why do you think your uncle didn't consult you before sending a letter to Joe?" Russ asked.

Taken aback by the question, which seemed to come out of nowhere, she said, "I suppose because he didn't want an argument."

"You would have vetoed the idea?"

"I'm not sure at this point. I think I might have—at least at first. After I thought it over, I don't know. What he told me altered my entire past from the way I always believed it to be. That's quite a shock."

"So you think in the end you would have agreed that the letter be sent."

Slightly annoyed, she said, "I told you I don't know. Why do you keep asking?"

"Just curious."

Okay, but why was he curious? she wondered. Somehow the questions had been a tad off-kilter. Disturbed, she drew into herself. Since he said nothing more, they continued walking in silence.

When they finally reached the Haskell house, she'd changed her mind about inviting him in. Which was just as well since, after seeing her to the door, he brushed his lips over hers with a "See you tomorrow," and was down the porch steps before she'd closed the door behind her.

Climbing to her room with a heavy heart, Mari tried to sort through the evening. What had gone wrong, and when? His questions on the walk home had been all but confrontational. Why?

In her room, undressing, Mari found an answer. His father. Lou Simon was in New York with Joe Haskell, and he was Haskell's attorney. It had crossed her mind before that a lawyer might view with suspicion her tentative claim to being Isabel's daughter, since she had no real proof. That possibility connected with Russ's father made her wonder for the first time whose side Russ was on.

Before this evening she hadn't really thought about there being two sides where Russ was concerned. How naive she'd been!

Hadn't she asked herself before about the coincidence of Russ showing up in Nevada and then being so conveniently on hand when she reached Mackinac? A pang shot through her chest. Was it coincidence or had he been sent to Nevada, then here, by his father?

The tears didn't start until she remembered their time in the cupola. How could she have been so wrong about him? After Danny Boy, she knew better than to trust any man, but Russ had somehow got past her defenses. Once her storm of crying abated, though, it occurred to her she might, after all, be misjudging him. Was it fair to condemn him without asking him if what she'd conjured up had any truth to it? Clinging to this fragile hope, she was finally able to sleep.

Even closed windows failed to keep the perfume of the blossoming lilacs out of Russ's bedroom, the last scent he wanted anywhere near him. It was obvious his questions had antagonized Mari. He realized now that may have been an unconscious decision on his part. If she got angry with him, that pretty well killed the chance of any lovemaking. While he'd urgently wanted to be with her, Russ knew he couldn't face himself if he didn't clear things up between them first. Since he'd been unable to make the confession, he might well have used the questions to distance them.

Tomorrow morning, he promised himself. This has gone on long enough. Too long. She deserves to know what I got myself mixed up in.

Russ figured he should notify his father first, and decide to call him before going to see Mari in the morning.

Only then did he fall into a troubled sleep.

In the morning, his father didn't answer his cell phone. Russ left a message with the answering service for him to call as soon as possible, and took his own cell phone with him before he set out to meet with Mari. When he arrived at Joe's, Pauline opened the door and told him Mari wasn't up yet.

"Come and have breakfast while you wait," she invited. "Diana and I have already had our waffles, but she has plenty of batter ready and waiting. I'll run up and check on Mari."

Since he hadn't yet eaten, he made his way to the kitchen, recalling with anticipation Diana's peerless waffles. He'd just finished a plateful when his cell phone rang.

"What's up, Russ?" his father asked from the other end.

Involuntarily, Russ glanced at Diana. She nodded and pushed through the swinging door, leaving him alone in the kitchen.

"It's a long story," Russ said.

"So get started."

Russ did his best.

Mari had been awake when Russ arrived. She'd cracked open her bedroom door and heard Pauline invite him to breakfast. What am I going to say to him? she asked herself. Unsure, she quickly showered and dressed, but when she was done, she still hadn't made up her mind what to do.

Deciding Diana was probably feeding him breakfast at the kitchen table, considering how welcome he was in this house, Mari chose to go down the back stairs, which led to the kitchen. When she was near the bottom, she saw the door was ajar, and she heard Russ's voice.

"Listen, Dad," he was saying, "I did what you asked."

Mari froze for a moment. Was his father here?

She inched down to the last step and peered through the crack. No, Russ was on the phone.

"Of course Mari doesn't know—why should she? She thinks I'm Mr. Straight Arrow." Stunned as she was by his words, she hardly noticed the bitterness in Russ's tone.

Her worst-case scenario about him was true. Blinking back tears, she fled back the way she'd come as quietly as she could. She'd been in her room for only a minute when someone tapped on the door.

"Mari, are you awake?" Pauline called. "I heard your shower running a little while ago."

Thinking fast, Mari kicked off her shoes and slid under the covers, pulling them up to her chin. "I did take a shower, but it didn't help this terrible headache I have," she said, unshed tears roughening her voice. "I'm back in bed and I think I'll rest till it goes away."

Pauline opened the door and looked in. "I'm sorry you're not feeling well. Can I get you anything?"

"No, thanks. I have medicine."

"I came up to tell you Russ is here."

"Oh, dear, my head hurts too much to see anyone. Would you please tell him so? Maybe tomorrow."

Pauline nodded and closed the door. Mari eased from the bed, smoothed the covers back into position and reached for the quilt on the rack near the footboard. Then she stretched out again and pulled the quilt partly over her, suspecting that Diana would be coming by to ask if she could bring her something to eat.

Telling lies was more trouble than being truthful, Mari thought.

Sure enough, a few minutes later Diana knocked at her door and then looked in on her, refusing to be fobbed off with Mari's, "I'm not hungry."

"I'll fix you some milk toast," the cook insisted. "That's what my grandmother always made for us kids when we were sick. And tea. Tea is good for headaches."

Feeling more guilty by the minute for putting her to extra trouble, Mari stayed where she was until the milk toast and tea arrived on a tray, which Diana set on the bedside table. "Drink the tea while it's hot," she said before leaving.

Mari sat up. She really wasn't hungry; what she'd overheard on the back stairs had taken her appetite away. But she felt obligated to at least try the milk toast, something she'd never even heard of. It turned out to be buttered and sugared toast with hot milk poured over it. Though mushy, it tasted much better than it looked.

After finishing the tea as well, Mari tried to think what to do next. All she really wanted was to be back at the Crowely Ranch. She missed her uncle and Willa, too. How she longed to talk to them. The nearest phone, she knew, was in the upstairs sitting room.

Her watch told her it was nine, which meant it was only six o'clock in Nevada. She hated to call before seven there. Since she was supposed to be suffering with a headache, she could hardly go downstairs to pass the time, so she was stuck up here for an hour. When her room began to feel like a cell, Mari padded down the hall to the sitting room, where she opened the French doors to the balcony. The fresh morning breeze carried the scent of lilacs, making her sigh. Would she ever be able to smell them again without thinking of Russ?

Sitting in a chair, she picked up a magazine and leafed through it without being able to concentrate on what she saw, much less read. By six-thirty Nevada time, she couldn't stand to wait any longer and lifted the phone.

''Crowleys','' Willa's familiar voice said.

''Thank heaven you're there,'' Mari blurted.

"Came over early to fix Stan breakfast, seeing as how they called him last night to come help out at the casino today. The bartender wound up in jail."

Mari heard the words without them quite registering. "Oh, Willa, I'm so miserable," she cried.

"Find out you ain't a Haskell?"

"No, not that, it's Russ Simon. He's been spying on me for his father, and all the time I thought he—well, liked me."

"Whoa there. Russ is the young man who bought Lucy, right? What's he doing on that island you went to? And what's this about his father?"

Mari told her the story, leaving out only what had happened in the cupola and on the boat. "He—he betrayed me," she wailed. "I want to come home."

"What's stopping you?" Willa asked.

Nothing was, Mari decided. Nothing at all.

"I'll get a flight to Reno as soon as I can," she told Willa.

Russ went home to change to work clothes, then headed for the stables, planning to spend the day with his Blues. He felt let down after his hard-won decision to tell Mari the truth, only to be balked because she wasn't feeling well. His father hadn't been happy with the news, but had finally accepted Russ's decision, saying it really didn't make any difference in the long run.

Russ hadn't bothered to try to make his dad understand just how much difference it made to him to stop living a lie. Mari deserved the truth, even if she never wanted to see him again after he told her.

He'd call around noon to see if she felt better. If he couldn't talk to her, he'd give Pauline the message he'd forgotten to leave earlier. His father had told him a lab technician would arrive on the island today to take samples from Mari. Bad timing, if Mari didn't feel well, but Russ knew she wanted to get it over with. Damned if he, like her, wouldn't be glad when everything was settled.

He smiled wryly, hoping the results would surprise the hell out of his mistrustful father.

Chapter Ten

Mari had no sooner finished her call to the island airport when she heard the doorbell ring. Russ? Even though she hoped not, her heart leaped. Moments later there were footsteps on the stairs.

Figuring it must be Pauline, Mari stepped out of the sitting room. "Are you looking for me?" she asked.

"A laboratory technician is here with orders from Mr. Haskell," Pauline told her.

Mari had forgotten all about the testing. "I'll slip on my shoes and be right down," she said.

"Are you sure you feel all right?"

Mari nodded. ''The medicine helped.'' She was beginning to believe she'd told more lies today than in her entire life to date.

Pauline had showed the technician, a fortyish woman, into Mr. Haskell's study. Once Mari entered and introduced herself, the woman nodded, saying,''I'm Betty. What I'm here to do will only take a few minutes. Have you been told about the tests?''

''Yes. I'm glad you're here.'' At last Mari was able to say something truthful. She desperately wanted it all to be over and done with, no matter what the outcome.

After she signed some papers agreeing to have the blood drawn and the DNA sample taken, Betty had her sit with her arm on the desk. Once the tourniquet was in place, Mari looked away, not caring to watch the needle go in or her blood drawn into the tube. Betty was so skillful that Mari scarcely felt the needle. Taking the DNA sample wasn't painful, either, and the entire process lasted no more than ten minutes.

''You understand the results will be sent to Mr. Haskell,'' Betty said as she packed up to leave. ''As I explained, that was in one of the papers you signed.''

Mari nodded.

After the lab tech was gone, Pauline hovered solicitously. Mari took a deep breath and readied what was if not a lie, then a half one. "I'll be flying back to Nevada this afternoon," she said. "I've just been waiting to have the tests done."

"Goodness, and you not feeling well."

"I'm better. I'm sure I'll be fine."

"Are you certain? Would you like some help packing?"

Mari touched Pauline's arm. "Thanks, but I'll manage. You've been very good to me. You and Diana both. I've really appreciated your kindness."

"As to that, we're sorry to see you go. Nothing livens up a house like young people."

Hurrying as fast as she could, Mari was able to make the next flight to the mainland, and from there caught a commuter flight to Chicago. At O'Hare Airport she was lucky enough to get on a plane to Reno as a standby passenger. Much as she'd hated to use the one "emergency" credit card she carried, she'd felt she had to. No way could she remain on the island any longer.

How foolish of her to allow herself to be charmed by a man again. How could she ever have imagined she was falling in love with Russ? From the very beginning, his only interest in her had been to discredit her. For that matter, why had she ever listened to Uncle Stan in the first place and gotten mixed up in the situation?

The only shred of sympathy she had was for Mr. Haskell, who she felt sorry for. She didn't believe it had been his idea to have Russ spy on her. More than likely it was his attorney friend, Russ's dad, who'd concocted the scheme. Lawyers tended to be suspicious. But that didn't excuse Russ's part in the masquerade.

By the time the plane set down in Reno, near midnight, Mari was exhausted. She had gone over and over everything that had led up to her stay on Mackinac Island so many times that it began to seem to her that people had been lying to her all her life.

On the way to the ranch in her uncle's pickup, she pretended to sleep so she wouldn't have to talk to him. She felt as though she wanted to crawl in a hole and pull it in after her.

When Mari woke in the morning, for a moment or two she was disoriented, then the reality of being home again seeped into her. As much as she'd longed to be back here, she really didn't feel any better now that she was. After eating the toast Willa insisted on fixing for her, and downing a cup of coffee, Mari made a beeline for the stables, feeling that the company of horses was all she could tolerate right now.

She didn't want to talk to anyone. Or listen. Willa was a dear and wise friend, one she'd shared her troubles with before, but Mari wasn't ready to share anything with anyone.

She saddled Tennille and rode out into the bright day. The temperature was already heading for the high eighties and Mari was conscious of the dryness and heat after being on the cool and moist island.

This is what I love, she told herself. I'm a true high-desert rat. I don't belong anywhere else. Stan had taught her to ride, but Blanche had been the one who'd identified the native trees and plants, insects and animals, and passed along her philosophy of helping others. Which was why Mari had rescued the estray mare, Lucy, following her aunt's tendency to adopt every stray she ran across.

Lucy had led to meeting Russ, but Mari refused to go down that mental road.

Was I just another stray to Blanche? she wondered. An orphan someone had to look after? The thought depressed her. Certainly her birth mother had qualified as one of Blanche's strays. Which reminded Mari of the question Russ had asked her: would Stan remember if Blanche had ever said what bus Ida had gotten off in Reno?

Even as Mari filed the question away to ask her uncle Stan, she was disgusted at herself for allowing Russ to seep back into her thoughts.

I won't think ill of Blanche, she vowed. I won't be angry at her for not telling me we weren't blood relations. I know she loved me, and whatever she withheld about my birth from me she believed to be in my best interests. Maybe it actually was. Nothing that has happened since Russ showed up here to buy Lucy is Aunt Blanche's fault.

Actually, it's not Uncle Stan's, either. He loves me and was trying to help me, not hurt me. I wish he hadn't contacted Mr. Haskell without my knowledge, but that's beside the point. It's not fair to blame my adoptive parents for any of this. I've no one to blame but myself for believing in Russ. Won't I ever learn?

"Why aren't we born with horse sense?" she asked Tennille, who merely flicked an ear, no doubt secure in the knowledge of having it herself.

When Mari got back to the ranch house, Willa was gone, leaving a note on the table telling her that lunch fixings were in the fridge. Since Stan was still filling in at the casino for the errant bartender, Mari would be alone at least until late afternoon.

Wandering through the familiar rooms, she felt restless enough to climb the walls. She'd taken care of what chores needed doing in the stables, and the house was neat and clean. Since she hadn't known when she'd return, her riding students had been referred to another instructor. What was there to do?

When she reached what Blanche had always called her workroom, containing a hodgepodge of craft items and yarn, Mari made herself go in and look around. After Blanche had died, she'd gone through her aunt's clothes and given what was wearable to a local charity, but she'd left this small room alone because it reminded her so acutely of her adoptive mother.

Taking a deep breath, Mari forced herself to start sorting things. She found a canister of odds and ends of lost jewelry never claimed by casino patrons that Blanche had brought home. There was nothing of particular value inside, but as a child Mari had loved to play with the unmatched earrings and other pieces. With a sigh, she set it aside in the charity pile, started to pick up a skein of yarn and then paused, remembering something triggered by the jewelry in the canister.

Two days before Blanche had gone to the hospital, where she'd died, she'd presented Mari with a pendant. Where was it now?

"This is yours by right," her aunt had said. "I should have given it to you long ago." She'd smiled. "Now the time's short—better late than never, right?"

Mari, worried sick about her aunt's congestive heart disease, had barely glanced at the pendant in the little jewelry box as she thanked her, being careful with her hug because Blanche was having so much trouble breathing.

When I find that pendant I'll wear it in her memory, Mari decided. Most likely she'd stuck it somewhere in her bedroom.

Finding the box in a dresser drawer, she opened it and removed the pendant. It looked to be silver, but if so, it hadn't tarnished at all. Maybe platinum? Engraved in the metal was a flower of some kind. A close look revealed the heart-shaped leaves and tiny flowers of a lilac. Mari's eyes filled with tears. Because it was Blanche's last gift to her, she told herself. Which was true, but how could she deny the meaning lilacs had taken on for her?

She fastened the silver chain around her neck and tucked the pendant inside the V of her shirt.

Willa returned in the late afternoon, insisting on fixing the evening meal. "Got so used to cooking for Stan and you that I can't hardly recall how to make a meal for just me," she said.

"You know you don't have to spoil us," Mari said.

"Well, now, let's think about that. Maybe the good Lord intended me to move out here to the desert so you and Stan could get a decent meal now and then. He's no cook, and it ain't something you much enjoy, is it? Don't forget, you buy the groceries, so I do eat free. And in good company."

"I'm afraid I'm not such good company right now."

Willa patted her arm. "Nothing says a body has to jabber away to be good company." She cupped a hand to her ear. "Sounds like Stan's truck pulling up. I best get the rice on."

When they sat down to eat, Stan told a few casino stories before turning to Mari and saying, "You been mighty quiet since you got back."

Since she wasn't ready to talk about the island, she said, "You know they did that blood and DNA test on me, so there's nothing to discuss until Mr. Haskell gets the results. I already told you he'll be returning home in a few days.''

"He told me on the phone about his heart being bad.''

"Well, he's recovering.''

"Anything else?''

About to say no, she remembered what she meant to ask him. "Did Blanche ever say anything at all about where the bus my birth mother got off in Reno might have come from?''

Stan's brow furrowed. "Seems like she did. Got to cogitate for a bit.'' After several long minutes, he said, "Got it. Came off Highway 80, from the east, Blanche figured, on account of the arrival time. Ida never did tell her much, you know. 'Course, she was pretty sick, what with the pneumonia and all.''

The "all'' meaning me, Mari told herself. But she didn't see how Stan's information would help much. Why had Russ even asked the question?

Another question she'd never asked her uncle occurred to her, but she waited until dinner was over and she'd helped Willa with the dishes before confronting Stan in the living room, where he was watching TV.

She sat beside him on the couch and he turned down the volume. "Why didn't you or Blanche ever tell me the truth about my birth mother—that she was no relation to either of you?" she asked him.

"Blanche made me promise I'd never tell you."

"Why?"

"You see, at first, when you were little, she was always afraid someone would find out there was no blood relationship, and they might come and take you away from us." He smiled at her. "You were like God's gift to us, Mari, and we'd both have done anything to keep you. Blanche always wanted a kid, but we never had one—till you came along."

"After I was older, though, an adult—why not tell me then?"

"Blanche worried that you might get mad and go off somewhere. I tried to tell her you'd never do that, but she made me keep my promise. Then, after she died, I heard Joe Haskell on TV asking for his daughter Isabel to come home, and I got to thinking about Ida and how she wouldn't tell Blanche anything about herself. It could be, I told myself. What if our Marigold is Joe Haskell's granddaughter? I'd be cheating her out of being an heiress to millions. So I broke my promise and told you."

Mari didn't chide him for telling Mr. Haskell first. Stan had set the chain of events in motion because he loved her. She had nothing to blame him for. She had nobody but herself to blame for not questioning the coincidence of Russ first being in Nevada and then on Mackinac Island. She'd let herself be duped.

"You look mad enough to spit nails," Willa said when Mari came back into the kitchen.

"You were wrong about Russ," Mari told her. "He's far from harmless—he's as poisonous as one of your rattlers."

"You saying that 'cause he broke your heart?"

"My heart is not broken!"

"Could've fooled me."

"It's my pride, just like you said with Danny Boy."

Willa shook her head. "Ain't saying your pride's not hurt. Probably is. That slick-talking rat you went with afore didn't so much as touch your heart, though, and you know it. This last one did, I can tell. You think about it, gal. Got to be honest with yourself or things are never right."

"I hear you, but I still don't ever want to see Russ again. Or talk to him. If he calls, just tell him I'm not in."

Later, after Willa had gone home and Stan had

fallen asleep in front of the TV, Mari went to bed and waited in vain for Willa's Mr. Sandman to visit. The tears she'd told herself she'd never again shed over Russ came in a torrent before she finally slept.

For two weeks, each day passed much like the one before. Mari made sure never to answer the phone so she wasn't sure if Russ had tried to reach her or not. She refused to ask Willa if he'd called and Willa didn't offer to tell her if he had. Not that Mari cared. Stan was filling in at the casino while they tried to find a replacement bartender who suited them, so all the outside chores fell to Mari. She welcomed the task. The harder she worked, the less time she had to think and the quicker she'd fall asleep at night.

At midmorning the beginning of the third week, she'd just finished hauling manure from the stables to the field when she heard Willa hailing her from the house. "Mari, phone call."

Mari's heart leaped, but she shook her head. It couldn't be Russ, Willa wouldn't call if it was. Still, it must be an important call. At the back door she stripped off her work gloves and stepped out of what she called her manure boots.

"Mari Crowley here," she said into the kitchen wall phone.

"Lou Simon," the man on the other end told her.

Mari's back stiffened. The enemy.

"As you may know, I'm Joe Haskell's attorney."

"Yes." She knew her tone was clipped and ungracious, but so what?

"Joe asked me to let you know the results of the tests done while you were on Mackinac Island."

Despite her determination to show no emotion, she broke in ask, "How is Mr. Haskell?"

"Doing very well. As I was saying, the results of these tests suggest there may be a relationship involved here. To be quite certain, I've arranged for another test to be done in Reno this afternoon. I realize this is short notice, but I'm sure you appreciate that everyone concerned wants an end to the waiting."

Mari could hardly credit what she'd heard. A relationship? Did that mean she might be Isabel's daughter, after all?

Lou Simon went on to tell her when and where in Reno she was to go for the tests, ending with,

"I've arranged for a limo to pick you up and take you there. Expect the car promptly at noon."

Mari told him she understood, but apparently failed to convince him, because he asked if she wanted him to repeat the instructions.

Collecting herself, she said, "That won't be necessary, thank you."

When she hung up the phone, she stood frozen in place, her mind struggling to make sense of what she'd heard.

"What was that all about?" Willa's voice startled her. "You'd think I was one of my rattlers, the way you jumped," she added. "Goodness, gal, I've been right here in the kitchen all along. Bad news?"

"I—I don't know whether it's bad or good. I mean, it's just more tests they want done. In Reno, this time."

"The ones you had done back east didn't turn out?"

"Lou Simon said there 'may be a relationship involved,' if I'm quoting him right. You know how lawyers talk. The Reno tests are to make sure one way or the other, I guess."

Willa grinned. "Don't you believe it, gal. Lawyer, you say? The bad guy, Russ's father?"

Mari nodded.

"Heard enough lawyer lingo in my life—my nephew and his son both went that route. Here's what he meant. The tests already say you're Joe Haskell's granddaughter, but this man don't want to believe that, so he's having them done over."

Mari stared at her for a long moment before she began to laugh. When she could speak, she said, "Here I am in my manure clothes, smelling to high heaven, and you're telling me I'm an heiress?"

Willa nodded. "When are you supposed to go to Reno?"

Reminded, Mari glanced at the wall clock. "There's a limo coming at noon. I'd better get showered and changed."

By noon she was wearing a denim skirt with a pale blue shirt, a compromise between jeans and dressier clothes. Willa had tried to get her to eat some lunch, but all Mari could get down was a cup of tea.

When she heard the limo pull up outside, she grabbed her purse and exited. The driver was waiting, holding the back door open for her, and she folded herself inside, only then aware that there was another person in the back seat.

"Hello, Mari," Russ said as the chauffeur shut her in with him.

Her heart pounded and she could hardly breathe. Why did he still affect her so much when she despised him? It wasn't fair. After calming down a little, she demanded, "What are you doing here?"

"Accompanying you to Reno," he said.

She bristled. "Was your father afraid I wouldn't go otherwise?"

"It was my idea. We have to talk." He leaned toward her. "Mari, I—"

She help up a hand. "I don't want to hear one word of explanation from you. We both know there was no excuse for what you did, so there's no point in discussing it."

"At least listen—"

"No! I may be trapped in here with you, but I can always put my hands over my ears if I have to." She glared at him. "And I will, make no mistake."

She shifted position, moving as far away from him as she could manage. As she did, the pendant swung out from the V of her shirt.

Before she knew what he meant to do, Russ slid over and reached for it, bending to peer at the engraving. She didn't dare move, lest the pendant be jerked off the chain.

He was close, so close his scent was in her

nostrils, reminding her of what she needed to forget. Again she couldn't breathe.

"It's a lilac," Russ said, so softly she scarcely heard him. "Lilac lady."

Her heart turned over. For a moment she was back in the gazebo, surrounded by the scent of lilacs, and Russ was gazing at her with this strange yearning look in his eyes.... No! She wouldn't remember. She refused to remember.

That time was gone beyond recall. Russ had betrayed her and she could never forgive him.

Chapter Eleven

In the back of the limo. Russ shifted away from Mari. Once he'd discovered she'd left Mackinac without so much as a goodbye, he'd known she'd somehow learned of his double-dealing, so her overt rejection and her refusal to listen to him wasn't a surprise. Since his attempts to call her never got him past Willa, he hadn't expected Mari to greet him with open arms, but he had hoped she might remember what they'd meant to one another on the island. Had he been the only one— as his father put it—smitten?

He couldn't help but be reminded of Denise

bailing out of their marriage without even giving him a chance to succeed with the horse farm. She'd rejected not only their marriage, but him as well. If Mari cared at all about him, wouldn't she be willing to hear him out?

Apparently he'd made another misjudgment.

While he'd been willing to explain himself, he certainly wasn't going to beg to be heard. To hell with that. He crossed his arms over his chest, staring straight ahead. If she wanted to talk she'd have to speak first.

She didn't, and since he'd asked the limo driver earlier not to make conversation, the rest of the drive to Reno took place in silence. When they arrived at the building where the lab was located, the driver parked, got out and opened the door for Mari. She exited, and the driver looked inquiringly at Russ, who shook his head. Let her find her own way to the damn lab; he had no intention of escorting her. After she disappeared inside the building, though, Russ got out on his side of the limo and walked around to the back, where the driver stood with one foot on the bumper.

"Quiet ride," the driver commented after a moment.

"Yeah."

The driver shrugged. "Women, who can figure?"

As he spoke, a blonde walked briskly past them, a striking young woman with long legs, a short skirt and a tight T-shirt. "'Course," the driver added when she was out of sight, "when one comes along like that, it reminds a guy why he don't want to live without 'em."

Russ had eyed the blonde, too. What male alive wouldn't have noticed her? But she hadn't had Mari's spectacular hair, her amber eyes, her grace of movement. In short, the blonde might have been sexy, but she wasn't Mari. So she didn't really interest him.

He nodded at the driver and strode off in the opposite direction from the one the blonde had taken. The day was hot, though the dry air made the heat tolerable. He thought his Blues would do well out here, but he wasn't so sure about himself. And he wasn't referring to the weather.

By the time he returned from his long walk, Mari was back inside the limo. The driver held the door open for him and Russ slid in. "Everything get done?" he asked her as the driver pulled from the parking lot.

"Yes," she snapped. "You can report to your

father the subject was cooperative and the lab tech swift and efficient.''

''I told you, I'm here on my own.''

She cast a disbelieving look at him.

He couldn't leave it like this, but what to do? An idea struck him. He leaned forward to speak to the driver. ''Pull over to the curb for a bit, okay?''

When the limo was no longer in motion, Russ said to Mari, who was obstinately looking the other way, ''Would you like to drive up to Winnemucca and see your father's grave?''

Her head whipped around and she stared at him. ''My father's grave? What are you talking about?''

''His name was Elias Grant, right?''

She nodded.

Russ spoke as bluntly as possible, sure that was the only way to reach her. ''Well, do you or don't you want to see where he's buried?''

Mari tried to collect her scattered wits. In some secret part of herself she'd cherished the hope that she'd one day find her father since she had always thought of him as still alive. ''I—I—yes,'' she stammered. ''But how did you find where he was?''

''We're going to Winnemucca,'' Russ told the

driver. "You'll have to inquire locally once we get there because I'm not sure where the cemetery is."

"No problem," the man said. "It's in the center of town."

Mari fidgeted, waiting for Russ to answer her question. She'd vowed not to talk to him unless she had to, but this changed things.

"After your uncle sent the copy of the birth certificate, Haskell Enterprises hired a private investigative firm to search for Elias Grant," Russ said. "I had nothing to do with this, believe it or not."

She hadn't thought so, but she wasn't about to tell him that. "How in the world did they find him? I asked my uncle if Blanche had told him anything more about Ida Grant, but all he could remember was Blanche had decided that Ida must have gotten off the bus coming west on Highway 80. Winnemucca is east of Reno, of course."

He nodded. "The investigators turned up Isabel's divorce from Mort Morrison a year before he was killed in a racing accident. The address under her signature was Winnemucca, Nevada. So they started asking around in Winnemucca, and they found Isabel, known locally as Ida, had lived with a local rodeo rider named Elias Grant until he was killed in a fall from a horse. One of the women they talked to said Ida was 'real pregnant' when that happened, and she left Winnemucca soon after.''

Mari sighed. "Poor Isabel.'' Her mother? It certainly seemed likely. What rotten luck Isabel had had with men. Maybe it was hereditary. A thought struck her. "Was she married to Elias Grant?''

Russ hesitated, then said, "The investigators didn't find any marriage recorded. " He paused, then added, "Apparently Elias was well liked around town.''

Realizing he was trying to offer her a shred of comfort, Mari accepted it in the spirit it was offered. At least her father had never deserted her mother except in death.

"It didn't take them long to discover all this,'' she said.

"Haskell Enterprises hires the best.'' His tone was wry. "Did you think your uncle was the first to contact Joe? There were six other claimants before you, Mari. This same investigative team exposed all six as, at the very least, mistaken. Can you blame my father for being suspicious of your claim?''

Startled—she was the seventh?—Mari said, ''I

would never have accepted the offer to fly to Mackinac Island if I didn't believe I might be Isabel's daughter.''

Russ nodded. ''Once I got to know you, I realized that.''

That was easy for him to say, now that he knew she probably was Joe's granddaughter. No, more than likely actually was. A tremor shook her. The realization was hard for her to grasp.

''Is he really all right? My—'' She couldn't yet bring herself to say ''grandfather.'' ''Mr. Haskell, I mean.''

''He has to go back for bypass surgery, but, yes, he's as all right as he can be right now.''

''I have to think about all this,'' Mari said, leaning back in the seat and closing her eyes. Here she was vindicated, she and Uncle Stan, and the only emotion she felt was confusion. She was glad to know who she was, but underneath all that, she was still basically Mari Crowley. Becoming Mari Haskell would take some doing.

Russ didn't try to talk to her again until they reached Winnemucca and the driver pulled into the cemetery. It didn't take long to find the gravestone. Mari stared down at the incised rider on a bucking horse gracing the top of the granite slab.

Underneath was written The Last Honest Cowboy.

Had her mother chosen the epitaph? Unexpected tears sprang to Mari's eyes and she blinked them back to look at her father's name, Elias Grant, and the dates of his birth and death.

There he lay, the last honest cowboy. Her father.

"A man couldn't ask for a better epitaph," Russ said from beside her.

Turning to him, Mari dissolved into tears. Russ's arms came around her, comforting, protective, and she sobbed on his chest, too stricken by her sudden onslaught of grief to care that she was allowing him to hold her. Soothed by his murmured words and the strength of his body, she eventually regained her composure and pulled away.

"I never knew him," she said. "I don't know why I'm so upset."

"All this has been hard on you, not knowing, never being sure. Now it's all over."

But was it really? "The tests today—" she began.

He waved his hand. "My father wanted those because he always asks for two opinions. In this case, Elias Grant has been found, and the divorce papers place Isabel in Winnemucca. Circumstantial evidence, he might argue, but damn convincing. As were the tests run back in Michigan by a very reputable lab.''

''We'd better be getting back to the ranch,'' Mari said, more unsettled than she'd ever been in her life. It felt as though the very sand under her feet was shifting. If only Russ... But no, that was over and done with. She could never trust a man who'd betrayed her.

When he'd held her as she wept, Russ had hoped it might be the beginning of a thaw. How right she felt in his arms. But he could tell by her words and her expression now that she was distancing herself again.

''We could stop for something to eat,'' he said. Seeing the refusal in her eyes, he hastily added, ''It's not really fair to let the driver go hungry.''

Her nod seemed reluctant.

''Fast food,'' she said. ''I don't want to waste time getting home.''

Russ remembered all too well when she didn't think having a meal with him was wasting time. Like their picnic in the meadow. Interrupted by tourists. Something always seemed to interfere with what was between them, but dammit, he refused to believe it was permanently destroyed.

"You left too soon," he told her. "I came over that morning to make my confession about what I'd done. But you'd already figured it out, and you faked that headache, didn't you?"

She raised her chin. "I don't care to discuss it. If we're going to eat, let's go and do it."

A fast-food place wasn't what he'd had in mind, especially not with the driver as a third party, so nothing personal could be said. But at Mari's insistence, that's where they went.

Back in the limo, he watched her settle into her corner and close her eyes, shutting him out. After a time she began to breathe deeply, and he realized she'd dozed off. She started to slump sideways and he quickly slid toward her, so she could rest against him. Murmuring something unintelligible, she nestled closer, her eyes remaining closed. He smiled slightly, anticipating how upset she'd be when she woke up and found where she was. In his arms.

Dammit, she was where she belonged, as far as he was concerned.

After a time he began to whisper to her. "I bought that ranch property up the road from you—the old Curwith Ranch. You thought I was lying about wanting Nevada land, but I wasn't, though I might not have gotten around to looking for any that soon if my dad hadn't laid the spying trip on me."

She shifted position slightly, but her eyes stayed shut, so he went on.

At first Mari thought she was dreaming about Russ whispering in her ear. He told her about the Nevada ranch he'd bought, of how well he expected his Blues to do out here, about hiring ranch hands. He was so close his warm breath tickled her ear.

"...collect Lucy," he was saying. "I've got the perfect stud for her. Let's hope she likes him better than you do me right now."

Mari blinked, slowly awakening. It *was* Russ she was hearing. Where was she? Held close. Warm and safe. In Russ's arms? With a start she came fully awake and jerked away from him, turning to give him a glare.

"Hey, you fell asleep on me. I didn't have a thing to do with it," he objected.

She recognized that might well have been the truth. "You said something about Lucy, didn't you?"

He smiled. "So you did hear me. I was telling you now that I've bought Nevada property, I'll be coming to collect Lucy soon. I need to get the men I've hired settled in first."

Since she'd come to believe all his talk of a Nevada ranch and Lucy being a Blue was part of his masquerade, she couldn't hide her surprise. "I thought I was dreaming," she said. "You really did buy that ranch up the road from me?"

He nodded. "I've needed to expand for some time, and there's been a growing market for draft horses here in the west. Nevada's perfect."

"But I thought—" she began, then shut up.

His raised eyebrow told her he understood what she didn't say. "Occasionally I do tell the truth," he told her.

To her annoyance, her heart gave a leap of joy that he'd be so near—not more than a couple of miles away. "If you've hired ranch hands, you probably won't need to be around much." The words were out before she thought, and she flushed. It sounded as though she cared.

He shrugged. "To the contrary, I expect to spend most of the summer fixing things up the way I want them."

Did that glance of his mean he was including her in the things he planned to "fix up"? She stiffened. Fat chance.

"I remember you showing me the Curwith Ranch," he said. "You'd lent me a chestnut gelding and you rode an Arabian mare—The Captain and Tennille, you said, named after singers your aunt Blanche admired."

Did he never forget anything?

"I also remember my first sight of you on the top of that fence rail. You took off your hat and waved it at your student, so I noticed your remarkable hair. I had already taken note of your no less remarkable butt."

Despite herself, Mari felt herself thawing. Thrown somewhat off guard, she said, "I'll bet you can't recall my student's name."

"Wrong. Yasmin."

"What is it with you—total recall?"

"As far as you're concerned. "

Realizing she was in danger of slipping back into their easy camaraderie, which she didn't intend to do—ever—she said coolly, "My recall may not be as precise as yours, but I do remember that everything you said and did was a pretense."

"You're wrong."

"So, okay, you bought the ranch I showed you. And I guess Lucy must really be a Blue. I just don't care to discuss it any further." She paused, then added in a softer tone, "Thank you for showing me my father's grave. If it hadn't been for all this, I might never have known where he was."

"Much less that he was the world's last honest

cowboy. I can't claim to be a cowboy, but I am, whether you believe it or not, basically honest.''

She frowned. "This is where I stop listening, so you may as well stop talking. Haven't you already told me enough lies?''

Russ spread his hands, turned away from her and didn't say another word until the limo pulled into the ranch driveway.

"Well—goodbye," she said to Russ as the driver opened the door for her.

"I'll be back," he told her.

She opened her mouth to tell him to forget it, but before she could he added, "For Lucy, that is.''

So he had the last word, after all, Mari thought in some annoyance. Naturally he'd meant for Lucy—why would she expect otherwise?

Chapter Twelve

The following week Mari got another call from Lou Simon.

"Joe wants to meet you," he told her. "He's sending his private jet to fly you here."

"To Mackinac Island?" she asked, trying to come to terms with this sudden announcement.

"No, he's moved to his Manhattan apartment to wait for his surgery date, so you'll be coming here. Would you also do him a favor and bring your lilac pendant with you?"

Taken aback, she asked, "My what?"

"Apparently you have a platinum pendant with

a lilac blossom engraved on it. Joe would like to see it.''

''Why, yes, I do.'' She left it at that, waiting for more of an explanation of why Joe Haskell was sending for her. She didn't get it.

''Then he'll be expecting you and the pendant tomorrow,'' Lou Simon told her, adding the time that the limo would pick her up to take her to the airport. Then he hung up.

''Mr. Haskell wants to meet me,'' she told Willa. ''Naturally, I wasn't told why.''

''That's obvious. The tests in Reno came out the same as those in Michigan. Added to what they learned about your father, Haskell knows you're his granddaughter and wants to welcome you into the family.''

''He's in New York City waiting to have by-pass surgery,'' Mari said.

''All the more reason to want to get to know you right away. Who can say how long any of us may live—and he's at risk.''

''Russ!'' Mari exclaimed. ''He had to be the one who told his father about my lilac pendant— you know, the one Blanche gave me before she died.''

''What's that have to do with anything?''

"Mr. Haskell wants me to bring the pendant with me. Why would he?"

"You can answer that yourself—the pendant must have some significance for Joe Haskell."

Mari nodded, the words that Blanche had said when she'd handed over the pendant echoing in her mind: *I should have given it to you long ago.* Where had the pendant come from originally? Had it been Ida's? "She was afraid," Mari said aloud.

"If you mean Blanche, yes, the poor dear soul. She loved you, gal, and feared to lose you. Hard on a body, that. Don't ever fall into the trap of trying to hold a love too close."

"I can't blame her."

"Why should you? Just remember never to do it yourself. Blanche aside, there's another thing to remember about love—it tends to be a free agent, choosing where it will, no matter whether a body wishes for it or not."

Mari frowned. "If you're back to my supposed broken heart, I was never in love with Russ Simon and I'm not now."

"And that's why you're so angry with him, 'cause you never did love him and don't now."

"No! I mean, yes, I'm angry about his treachery. Who wouldn't be? It has nothing to do with love.''

"Ah, well, it took me years to learn. Maybe I expect too much from a gal your age. Tell me, when are you leaving for New York?''

"The limo will be here at seven tomorrow morning.''

"Best we look over what you might want to pack. The city ain't the same as a summer island. I figure you might have to add to your wardrobe.''

Willa soon convinced Mari she had to go into town and buy at least one more outfit, assuring her this was a sufficient emergency to use the credit card. "You're the Haskell heiress, gal,'' she added. "You got to figure that in sometime.''

While she was in town, Mari stopped by the casino to tell Uncle Stan the latest turn of events.

He beamed at her. "I knew it. The minute I listened to Joe Haskell on TV, I got this hunch about you. Blanche may have broke me of gambling, but I was a good one in my day, and when us old gamblers get a hunch about a sure thing, the odds are dang good we're right.''

Driving home with the new clothes she'd bought, Mari mused that her uncle had been more excited than she was. Her main feeling was numbness. It was as though some other Mari had been proved right in her claim that Isabel had been her mother. Though she was happy for Mr. Haskell—would she ever get accustomed to thinking of him as her grandfather?—she couldn't quite grasp what it meant to her.

Everything had come too fast. Stan's disclosure that Blanche was no blood relation to her. The discovery that Mari's birth mother, Ida, was actually Isabel Haskell. Seeing her father's grave and learning that at the very least he'd been an honest cowboy. If that wasn't enough, in the midst of all this she'd met the man she'd believed might be the only one in the world for her, only to be rudely disillusioned.

The evening meal turned out to be a festive celebration. Willa had made her special New England boiled dinner and baked an apple pie. Stan uncorked the champagne saved for a special occasion.

"To our own Marigold, the missing Haskell heiress," he said, raising his glass. "May she live long and happily."

"Money won't do it. She ain't going to be happy lest she learns to follow her heart," amended Willa.

Stan shrugged, and they all took a sip of champagne.

Mari smiled and did her best not to show her doubts. Not about being a Haskell—she'd pretty much accepted she was. But she was also a Grant, wasn't she? However, in her heart she still felt like the person she'd been for all of her twenty-seven years—Mari Crowley.

The flight to Kennedy Airport in New York and the limo drive to Joe Haskell's penthouse apartment went past in a blur. The first time she came out of her daze was when Mr. Haskell held out his arms to her and she walked into his hug. He held her away and brushed his hand lightly over her hair.

"I knew you were Isabel's girl the minute I saw the color of your hair in that picture," he said. "Had to let the legal boys satisfy themselves, but in my heart, I knew."

Mari tried to force words past the lump in her throat. "I—I—Mr.—"

"Grandpa Joe," he said simply.

"Grandpa Joe," she repeated, surprised at how easy it was to say. "I can't tell you what it means to actually have a grandfather."

The man standing by the door cleared his throat, and Joe glanced at him.

"My dear," he said to Mari, 'this is my life-

long friend Lou Simon, who worries about me far
too much.''

Seen in person, the enemy didn't look anything
like an ogre. Not quite as tall as Russ, with gray
hair rather than black, he smiled at her as benev-
olently as her grandfather had. His eyes, though,
green as his son's, remained watchful. ''We meet
at last, Ms. Grant,'' he said.

The name startled her for a moment. Was that
who she was? ''Please call me Mari,'' she murmured.

''No wonder he was smitten, Joe,'' Lou Simon
said.

Grandpa Joe chuckled. ''Russ knew who she
was long before you'd admit it. Lawyers stop seeing with their hearts early on.''

''My son's an attorney, too,'' Lou reminded
him.

Joe shook his head. ''Get over it. He raises
horses. Profitably and happily, I might add.'' He
turned to Mari. ''Don't mind Lou and me. We
enjoy sparring.''

''I'll be going along,'' Lou said. ''I'm glad
you're here, Mari. Joe needs you.''

Her grandfather's housekeeper, an older woman named Rose, showed Mari to her room so she

could freshen up. Then Mari returned to the living room, where Grandpa Joe was waiting.

"I know you must be tired," he told her, "but I do want to see that pendant, if you don't mind."

Mari unclasped it from around her neck and handed the pendant and chain to him. He studied it, plucking a small magnifying glass from his shirt pocket for a closer look. After a time he nodded and looked at her. She saw the glint of tears in his hazel eyes as he handed the pendant back to her.

"If I had any doubts, and I admit to none," he said, "this would be the clincher. Many years ago, my dear wife, who was especially fond of lilacs, had this platinum pendant made for your mother's tenth birthday. Isabel always said it was her favorite gift, since she shared her mother's love for lilacs. She took the pendant with her when she ran off with that blasted drummer." He smiled wryly. "Though you're my beloved granddaughter under any circumstances, I must tell you I was relieved when your father turned out to be someone other than Mort Morrison."

"Elias Grant was the last honest cowboy," Mari said.

Joe nodded. "They told me about the inscription. A man couldn't ask for more."

"I don't have any pictures of him," Mari said, "but I suspect I may resemble him, since I don't look like any pictures of Haskells I've seen."

"Russ told me you found Isabel's portrait in the cupola room. Which reminds me. It was none of my doing that Lou roped his son in on vetting you. You must know by now why Russ consented to do such a thing."

Mari was tempted to tell him she didn't care to know, but she wasn't well enough acquainted with Grandpa Joe yet.

"We all make mistakes—too often with those we love the most. Mine was with Isabel, Lou's with Russ. When the boy refused the offer to join Lou's law firm because he wanted to raise horses, Lou disowned him. So, what I figure is when your uncle's letter came, Lou killed two birds with one stone. He wanted to protect me, and at the same time he saw a way to offer an olive branch to his son without losing face. The result was he asked Russ to check you out."

"Russ didn't have to agree!"

"Oh, but he did. He must have been quite aware of what Lou's request really was. To say no would have been to reject his father all over again. Black-and-white is all very well, my dear, until you come to family issues—this was a gray area.''

Mari couldn't help saying, "I hate to be lied to.''

He nodded. ''No doubt as much as Russ hated lying to you.''

Though she understood what her grandfather was trying to tell her, she wasn't sure she accepted it.

''But here I am, lecturing to you on the very evening of our happy reunion. Why don't we save any further revelations until breakfast?'' He rose and held out his hand.

Mari got up from her chair, taking his hand, and once again he hugged her. This time she hugged him back with more than mere politeness. She was beginning to like her grandfather.

''For a while I was sorry Uncle Stan wrote that letter to you,'' she said, ''but now I'm not.''

Alone in her bedroom, Mari tried in vain to sort out her thoughts, but they were in such a jumble she gave up and started to get ready for bed. She was reaching for her nightgown when she smelled the lilacs. Since she'd already taken in her surroundings, she knew there were none in the room. Finally she found the source—a lilac sachet tucked in the dresser drawer with the clothes the housekeeper had unpacked.

So, of course, Mari dreamed of Russ. They were on his sailboat heading for the Mackinac Bridge, gleaming high above them. When she protested that there'd be fog ahead, he smiled and pulled her to him.

"There's always fog ahead," he told her.

Just before they plunged into grayness, she woke up. After she settled down into sleep again, she dreamed once more. She and Russ were in a gazebo, but it wasn't his father's. It looked like the one on the Adams Ranch in Carson Valley, where her friends lived. In the evening darkness he pointed to a bright star. "That's the one I'll come from to rescue you," he said. "Watch for me." Then he was gone, and she was alone in a chilling night breeze.

When she woke in the morning, the shards of the dreams clung to her. In an effort to dispel them, she told herself that, however romantic the legend of Arch Rock might have been, she was not a trapped Chippewa maiden needing rescue, and Russ certainly wasn't one of the Sky People. He was Lou Simon's son. Though she had to admit the elder Simon wasn't the ogre she'd expected, she wondered if she'd be able to like him.

At breakfast, Grandpa Joe was much more solemn than he'd been the evening before. After greeting him, she asked how he felt.

"I'm fit enough for the bypass, my dear, and the date is set for a week from now. I was determined to get you here before then and I have."

"So soon," she said. "The operation, I mean."

"I've been putting it off," he admitted. "Finally they told me if I didn't have the bypass done, the next time my heart acted up would be the last. 'You waited pretty late, Joe,' Doc Vanable said. 'So this is a case of better late than never.'"

"That's what Aunt Blanche said when she gave me the lilac pendant," Mari told him, then related the whole story.

"I'm glad you had loving parents," he said. "I've only myself to blame for not trying to find you earlier."

Mari found that after breakfast she was scheduled, with Joe, to meet with not only Lou Simon, but other attorneys from his firm. "No one going under the knife can be sure of survival," Joe explained. "It's best you have some idea of what responsibilities you may be facing."

She couldn't prevent her alarm from showing,

and he reached over to squeeze her hand. "Don't worry."

That afternoon, his secretary, Natalie, took her shopping in stores Mari had heard of but never been in. No mention was made of cost as Natalie talked her into buying far more than Mari thought she needed, convincing her she definitely would require the clothes for various events she'd be expected to attend.

Since Grandpa Joe was resting before dinner, in the late afternoon Mari retreated to her room for a rest herself. Being a Haskell was going to change her life far more than she'd realized.

As the week passed, Mari met so many people she had trouble keeping them straight in her mind. Natalie again took her shopping, for a watch Grandpa Joe insisted on giving her, plus shoes.

When Mari protested that he was spending too much on her, he said, "You must remember you're a wealthy young woman now. For one thing, you've inherited the trust fund I set up for Isabel years ago in case she ever did return." He named an amount that knocked Mari back on her heels. "I've also set up a monthly allowance for you." Again the sum rattled Mari.

"I—I don't need that much," she protested.

"Think about it, my dear. You now have the

means to pay off the mortgage Russ told me is on your uncle's ranch. If you'd like to have Lou set up a trust fund for your uncle to draw interest on, just let me know. I hope to meet Stan Crowley one of these days, for I certainly owe him.''

The ranch free of debt? Mari could hardly imagine that.

She did enjoy her grandfather's company and the sightseeing trips she took under Natalie's guidance, but it all seemed unreal, so far removed from her horses and the ranch in Nevada. Of course, she wouldn't dream of leaving Grandpa Joe until after he had the heart surgery and was fully recovered. Nevada seemed so far away, so out of reach. She longed to be back, but that would have to wait.

Joe Haskell surprised his doctors by coming through the quadruple bypass with no problems and undergoing a smooth and rapid recovery. ''I told them I was too mean to die,'' he said to Mari when he was recuperating at home.

''You're not mean at all.''

His smile faded. ''But I was, my dear. More so than you can believe. It takes some of us a long time to learn life's lessons. ''

Which reminded Mari of Willa, and she told him all about her friend. Her grandfather was fascinated, and so she related more stories about Carson Valley and her friends there, fueling her own desire to return. Finally, toward the end of September, when it was evident her grandfather was in much better condition than he'd been before the bypass surgery, she mentioned her longing to go back to the ranch.

"Why, of course, my dear," he said. "You can visit your uncle anytime you wish. I'll arrange to have you flown to Nevada as soon as possible."

The word he'd used—*visit*—brought home to her the fact that she was a Haskell now, and so her life was not really her own. The thought was unnerving. Her grandfather expected her to live with him and she did want to spend time with her only blood relative, but she missed her uncle Stan, who'd been a father to her all her life. She also missed Willa. The ranch was home. Mari sighed, realizing she could no longer call it that.

"I hope you're happy here with me," Grandpa Joe said.

While she assured him she was, which was true enough, she didn't try to explain her feelings to him. And she certainly wouldn't admit to him or anyone how disappointed she'd been that Russ hadn't once come to Grandpa Joe's apartment since she'd been there. She knew he'd come to see him in the hospital, because Joe had mentioned it.

Was Russ deliberately avoiding her? She should have been happy about that, since she'd certainly made it clear she didn't want his company, but she wasn't. It was almost as though she missed him. Which was ridiculous.

Chapter Thirteen

Mari hadn't been back at the ranch for more than a day before she discovered Russ's purchase of the property up the road from hers was the talk of the valley. Her uncle had met him and pronounced him a right one.

"Knows what he's doing, no greenhorn," Stan said at their evening meal on the second day. "He's rebuilt the barn and has 'em working on the house."

"It was in pretty bad repair," Mari said, glad to have something neutral to comment on.

"He'll be over this week to pick up Lucy.

Asked did I think she'd go on a lead without any problem." Stan scratched his head, making gray tufts stand up. "Truth is, I don't know, since we never tried it."

"You're right. I got Lucy behind the fence by luring her in with oats. But it shouldn't be a problem."

"That's one stubborn mare," Willa commented. "Far be it for me to advise you about horses, but maybe you forgot how balky she can be when you want her to do something she don't have a mind to do."

"I imagine she's been on a lead sometime in her life," Mari said, but she was replying without really thinking what she was saying. Her mind was fixed on the fact that Russ would be coming to get Lucy. Mari would be seeing him, and she both longed to and dreaded it. Maybe she should try to be somewhere else when he arrived.

As if in answer, Willa said, "I'm thinking you best be around when the time comes for Lucy to leave here. That mare'll do more for you than for anyone else."

"She took to Russ," Mari said, recalling how he'd sweet-talked Lucy into good behavior.

Willa nodded. "People around here took to

him, as well. Saw him riding with Zed Adams the other day.''

"Charm does tend to get you places.''

Willa frowned. "So does ability. You're looking at that young man skewed.''

"Come on, Mari, you don't make a go of raising horses on charm,'' Stan protested. "You got a hate against him for some reason?''

Since she hadn't told Stan anything about her involvement with Russ, Mari shook her head. Deliberately changing the subject, she said, "Just who's the patsy around here?'' she asked him. "You accused me of being too softhearted when I brought strays home, but I sure wasn't responsible for that dog with six puppies out there in the shed.''

"Maisie was starving to death,'' Stan said. "Can't have that. I expect those pups'll make good hunting dogs—got to be some Lab in 'em. Might even make a profit selling 'em.''

"Her name's Maisie?''

He shrugged. "That's what she looked like to me—a Maisie. Just like that big dapple-gray looked like a Lucy to you.''

Mari grinned at him. "Can't argue with logic. But Lucy's a Blue, not a gray.''

"That's what Russ claims. Can't see it myself,

but he makes a good living raising whatever they are, so I don't argue.''

The very next day Russ arrived at the Crowley Ranch bright and early on a gorgeous black gelding. Mari was busy grubbing out the stables, but told herself firmly it made absolutely no difference if he was seeing her in her manure clothes. Wasn't he a horse person, too? Besides, she didn't care what he thought of her—not anymore. Unfortunately, her heart didn't seem to understand, because it sped up and something happened to her breathing.

''Hi, Russ,'' she said as lightly as she could. ''That's a magnificent black. What's his name?''

He swung off the gelding before answering. ''Black Knight, what else? Want a hand?''

She eyed him. His jeans and shirt had seen a lot of wear, she noticed as she looked him over. No matter what he wore, he was as gorgeous as Black Knight. ''Thanks, but you're not quite grubby enough,'' she told him. ''Besides, I've finished mucking out. Stan'll take care of the rest of it. They finally got another bartender at the casino, so he won't be working there as soon as the new guy gets trained.''

She knew she was babbling, telling him what

he probably already knew, but if she could keep a barrier of inconsequential words between them, maybe she wouldn't want so badly to touch him. "I suppose you've come to get Lucy."

"Right. I'm going to try to lead her back to my place."

"Give me a few minutes to change and I'll help you get a lead on her. There's coffee on in the kitchen. Muffins, too."

Without waiting for a reply, she strode to the back door of the house, stepping out of her boots and dumping her work gloves before going inside. In her room, she hurriedly changed into jeans and a T-shirt and ran a brush through her hair. Glancing in the mirror, she wished she'd at least put on lipstick earlier. To do it now would announce that she cared how she looked to Russ. She didn't!

He was sitting at the kitchen table finishing up one of the bran muffins Willa had baked the day before. Willa was at her own place this morning.

"Join me," he invited Mari. "You look like you could use a muffin. How's Joe?"

"In fine fettle when I left," she said as she poured herself coffee and slid into a chair across from him. "By the way, thanks for telling him about my lilac pendant—it meant a lot to him as a memento of Isabel."

"I had no idea there was a history to the pendant, so I can't take any credit. I happened to mention it to my dad, and he was the one who understood its significance."

Though Mari badly wanted to ask Russ why he'd bothered to discuss her pendant if he didn't know it was a Haskell artifact, she forced herself to stay quiet. Best to keep away from anything remotely intimate.

He grinned at her. "I can see you're dying to ask the obvious question. It's a long story, but I'll condense it. My dad and I get along now better than we have in years. I won't go into why—I'm sure you know. So we talk. When he asked me about you, for some reason I told him how much you loved lilacs, and I mentioned the pendant. He called Joe." Russ paused, then added, "I've always enjoyed watching you drink coffee."

Startled, she almost choked on a swallow. When she recovered, she told herself not to take anything he said as truthful. But what an odd thing to say if it wasn't true. She glanced at him, and the intensity of his gaze caught her unaware, trapping her, making her feel the sizzle of what she couldn't deny was still between them.

"The evening star is especially bright this month," he said softly.

Mari almost melted. Finally forcing her gaze away from him, she rose and announced, "Time to get Lucy on the road to her new home."

"You could saddle up and ride over with us."

She shook her head. "Too busy. Thanks, anyway."

He'd brought a lead rope and, after murmuring sweet nothings to Lucy, had no trouble fastening it to her bridle, or leading her through the fence gate.

He mounted Black Knight and set the gelding into motion. Lucy walked behind docilely enough until they passed Mari, who stood watching. At that point Lucy balked, refusing to move.

Since Lucy was a lot bigger than the gelding, Black Knight was forced to a halt. No amount of tugging or coaxing had any effect on Lucy. She just wasn't going anywhere.

"I think it's you," Russ told Mari finally. "Lucy doesn't want to leave you, and who can blame her?"

Because she couldn't think of any other solution, Mari saddled Tennille and rode up even with Russ's black. "See, Lucy, I'm coming, too," she said.

Russ urged Black Knight on again, and with Mari riding beside him, Lucy obligingly walked behind on the lead. Since the scheme was working, Mari realized she'd have to go all the way to Russ's new property to make sure Lucy wouldn't balk again.

"I told you she could be stubborn," Mari said.

"Looks to me as though you could go anywhere and she'd follow."

"Just don't call me if she won't let your stud— what's his name, by the way?—near her."

"King Arthur."

Disarmed, Mari chuckled. "He may demand a Guinevere rather than a Lucy."

"Arthur's more practical than romantic. He's got horse sense."

"I was just asking Tennille the other week why humans weren't lucky enough to be born with horse sense."

"Get any answer?"

She shrugged. "Horses keep their secrets well."

Though she realized she'd fallen into an easy exchange with Russ, endangering her determination to be aloof, she couldn't seem to back off. How she'd missed being with him!

Once they reached the old Curwith property, Mari was surprised by the improvements Russ had already made. As Stan had said, the new barn was already up, and men were working on the house.

Between the two of them, Russ and Mari managed to convince Lucy she wanted to go into a paddock. Mari dismounted, then stood and talked to her for a few minutes, feeding her a carrot she'd brought along.

"You'll like it here, Lucy. Russ'll take good care of you, and one of these days you'll get to be a mother and have the greatest, most magnificent foal in the whole world. A foal fit to carry a knight on its back once it's old enough, even though there are no knights anymore. A shame, don't you think?"

"Are you sure?" Russ asked.

She glanced at him. "Sure that there aren't any knights around? Positive."

"Then I guess I'm demoted. You'll have to let a mere commoner show you around the place."

Time to mount Tennille and get away. But instead, Mari found herself following Russ, listening, then responding to his enthusiasm as he told her what he planned to do.

"I'm temporarily living in that camper," he said, pointing.

"But that's Stan's," she blurted.

"Yeah, he offered to lend it to me. Your uncle's quite a guy."

Stan and Russ were buddies?

She'd been here far too long. Firming her resolve, she said, "I've got to be getting back."

He followed her to where the horses were tethered, and helped her mount Tennille. She was about to say goodbye when she saw him swing onto Black Knight.

"Take a short detour with me down to the creek," he said. "I want to show you something."

After hesitating for a moment, she agreed. Why not?

"It was there already, but really rackety. Rebuilt it myself." He sounded inordinately proud of whatever it was. "Like you with the gazebo, this is something I've always wanted."

They crested a small rise and he pointed ahead to the row of trees hugging the creek. "See that big cottonwood?"

She nodded.

"Whoever it was made the first one knew his trees—a perfect choice," Russ continued.

Finally seeing the light, she said, "We're talking about a tree house here, right?"

"Didn't I say so?"

"Not clearly enough."

"Just wait till you see it." He sounded as eager as a boy to show off the project he'd built.

When they reached the cottonwood, she peered through the leaves and saw what looked to be a structure a lot more elaborate than the scrap lumber platforms she remembered as a child. It not only had four walls and a roof, but two real windows, as well.

"Good heavens, you made it out of redwood," she commented.

"Wanted it to last. " He dismounted, jerked a rope hanging from the tree, and down came a ladder. "Climb up. "

Feeling like a kid again, Mari slid off the mare and pulled herself up the ladder into the interior of the tree house. Gazing around, she took note that he'd made two benches for furniture. A fuzzy green rug covered most of the floor. Just as she spotted the red telescope, Russ entered the tree house.

Noting what she was looking at, he said, "I always wanted one, and this seemed the perfect place to put it." He couldn't tell whether the telescope reminded her, as it did him, of their time in the cupola. "I focus through an open window."

"Don't the leaves get in your way?" Either her

voice sounded the least bit strained or it was wishful thinking on his part.

"I chopped off a few limbs for a clear view." He leaned down to peer through the finderscope. "Look, here's the Crowley Ranch."

She hesitated, but then moved to stand beside him and look into the eyepiece, close enough so he could catch a faint scent of lilac. The impulse to gather her into his arms was so strong he had to force himself not to move.

Mari lifted her head from the telescope and stared into his eyes. "So you're still spying on me," she snapped.

Anger shot through him. He gripped her shoulders. "That's nonsense and you know it. What's past is past."

But it wasn't past, neither the betrayal nor the need for her. He hauled her closer and his mouth came over hers in a kiss that held both the anger and the urgent desire roiling in him. For a long, desperate moment he felt no response, and then her body melted against his and her lips parted to welcome him. He could have shouted for joy that this bond between them hadn't been destroyed.

He deepened the kiss, tasting her while she tasted him, relishing the feel of her in his arms, wanting the moment never to end, while knowing he needed more, needed all of her. Now.

He felt her fingers threading through the hair at his nape, holding him to her. He cupped his hands under her butt, pressing her against his arousal, an invitation without words, and caught her moan of desire in his mouth. She wanted what he wanted. There was no reason to wait any longer.

Except one. He felt in his bones that if they made love with her still casting him in the role of bad guy, she'd be angry later—at herself and at him—driving them further apart. Mari had to come to terms with what he'd done at his father's bidding before he made love with her, or there'd be no future for their relationship.

Still holding her, he lifted his lips from hers. "I need to know one thing," he whispered. "Have you forgiven me?"

Mari stiffened, jerked from her daze of desire. Forgiven him?

Before she could try to pull away, he let her go, saying, "I take it you haven't." He stepped back, widening the space between them.

Then she understood. If she couldn't forgive him, he didn't want her. Angry and hurt at his abrupt rejection, she turned away from him, scrambled down the ladder, mounted Tennille and fled for home.

Why had she allowed herself to fall under his spell again? Even now, upset as she was, she yearned to be in his arms. It was clear she couldn't trust herself where Russ was concerned.

Chapter Fourteen

Willa was in the kitchen of the ranch house when Mari came storming in the back door. She tried to hurry past, but Willa took hold of her arm. "Young lady," she said, "I've had about enough of your carry-on. Sit you down. I'll fix some of my special mint tea and then we'll talk."

Mari, who'd done all the crying she intended to while in the stable tending to Tennille, didn't look directly at Willa, hoping to conceal her red eyes. "Carry-on?" she asked.

"You know very well what I mean. Sit you down."

Slumping onto a chair, Mari sighed and, while Willa bustled about getting the tea ready, tried to think of how to glide over what was troubling her. No one could help her, so it was useless to talk about the problem she had with Russ.

After Willa plunked the mug of tea before her, Mari leaned over, inhaling the minty scent.

"Drink it," Willa ordered. "Mint tea is good for the heart."

Involuntarily, Mari put a hand to her chest.

Sitting opposite her, Willa picked up her own mug and took a sip. "Nothing wrong with my heart, but it don't hurt to take precautions."

Fully intending to say there was nothing wrong with her heart, either, Mari found herself blurting, "I can't forgive him."

"Why not? To err is human, to forgive divine."

"Maybe so, but I hate liars, you know that. Russ betrayed me."

"From what you said your grandpa Joe told you, Russ did what he did because he felt obligated to his father for disappointing him."

Mari stared at her for a moment. "He didn't say exactly that."

"That's what he meant. Think about it. Russ allowed his father to pay his way through law school, then turned around and refused to practice law. Don't you think he felt guilty?''

"But Russ wanted to raise horses. He had a real struggle to succeed.''

"What you want to do, then doing it despite the odds, don't prevent guilt. I suspect his father was too proud to come right out and tell Russ he was sorry about casting him off, just like Russ felt too guilty to try to approach his father. Think of it in another way, gal—if it hadn't been for you, years may have gone by before they became reconciled. If ever. You were responsible.''

Mari took a couple swallows of mint tea while she tried to make sense of this. Willa had the strangest way of turning things head over heels.

"Lou Simon figured I was the seventh impostor—there'd been six before me who really were impostors," she said finally.

"Lucky seven, as Stan would say. Never saw a man as superstitious. Unlucky black cats, don't walk under ladders, knock on wood, wish on the first star—he believes it all. I told him the first star in the evening is often not a star at all, 'tis one of the planets, but did that change his mind?'' Willa shook her head.

"The evening star,'' Mari repeated. "Is it really a planet?''

"Right now 'tis Venus," Willa told her.

"Russ told me a Native American legend about the evening star."

"Always ready to hear a story, that's me," Willa said.

Mari told her how a maiden was loved by one of the Sky People, her father's cruel treatment, and how her lover rescued her by sliding down a ray from the Evening Star and bringing her back to his home in the sky.

"A romantic tale, don't you think?" Willa commented.

Mari sighed. "Yes, I suppose so, but those legends belonged to another time and another people."

"Don't forget that Venus, during another time and to another people, was the goddess of love."

"What's that have to do with the legend?"

"Goodness, what a dense gal you can be. Didn't I just say Venus was currently the evening star?"

"Oh." But Mari still didn't understand what point Willa was trying to make.

"You listen to me. What you got to do is ask your heart what it wants and then pay attention to the answer. Can't be happy otherwise."

Mari carried this advice around for the rest of

the day and finally took it to bed with her. It proved to be poor company, for it kept her awake.

The next morning at breakfast, she told Stan how Russ had built a tree house, wanting to get what had happened there out of her mind by presenting the tree house as though it had nothing to do with her. Just a building in a tree.

"I guess Russ never had a tree house when he was a boy," she finished.

"Yeah, that can stick with you, never getting what you long for. I finally got to understand I never would if I stayed a gambler. You see, compulsive gamblers don't really care if they win or lose—it's the game that counts. So you can't ever get what you long for, can you? All you can do is win or lose money. And it's mostly lose. So I quit." He smiled wryly. "'Course, it was either quit or Blanche'd kick me out—that played a part."

"I miss her."

"Yeah, we always will, I guess. But you got your grandfather now."

Willa came in the back door carrying eggs for them. "My dang chickens lay more'n I can eat," she grumbled as she stowed them in the fridge. "Stopped to look at the pups. They got their eyes open—pretty soon now they'll be out of that shed and underfoot.''

"Only going to keep Maisie," Stan said. "I already got Zed Adams interested in taking one of the pups. " He turned to Mari. "Speaking of Zed, I remember you, as a kid, always wanting a gazebo like the one on his ranch. You never did get one, just like Russ did without a tree house. But nothing's stopping you from having a gazebo built now that you're a Haskell.''

What he said was true. She could afford to build a gazebo on the ranch. "With lilacs," she said aloud. "Lilacs all around it."

Stan shook his head. "You and them lilacs. "

"Best get it done quick," Willa suggested, "seeing as how you're only here on a visit."

Visit. The word stuck in Mari's craw. Instead of going out with Stan to help with the morning chores, she lingered to talk to Willa.

"I can't help loving Grandpa Joe," she began.

"'Course not. He's your blood."

"He—well, he takes over. I know he thinks it's what's best for me, but that's not necessarily so. And I understand why he wants me with him instead of off in Nevada. I want to be there for him and yet live my own life, too. I'm just not sure how to go about it."

"You ain't got around to letting him know how you feel. You better. And soon."

"I keep telling myself I will, but then I think about Isabel and how they didn't get along. Look what happened there. I don't want to upset him."

"Joe didn't get where he is without being tough and aggressive. You got to remember you're a Haskell, just like he is. So was Isabel. You can't be passive with a man like Joe—he'll run right over you, like he tried to do with his daughter. By the sound of it, she chose not to stay and fight it out with him, but ran away. Be what your blood says you are—stand up to your grandfather and tell him no matter how much you love him, you have your life to live."

Mari sighed. Easier said than done.

"What about Russ?" Willa asked.

After all the "carry-on," as Willa put it, that Mari had done over Russ, how could she come right out and admit she'd been narrow-minded? Because she had been. "I guess you were right about my pride being hurt," she said finally.

"Pride's in the head. Got to listen to the heart."

"I don't know how to go about undoing what I've done."

"Get that dang gazebo built first."

"But—"

"Just do it. You'll see."

Stan came in the back door. "Hailed Russ's builder on his way past here," he said. "Man says he can have one of his workers here after lunch. Take less'n a week to get it done, he figures. How's that sound?"

It took Mari a moment to understand he was talking about her gazebo. When she did, she rushed over and hugged him. Having a gazebo at long last wouldn't solve her problem with Russ, but she was pleased at the thought of getting one. Is that what Willa had meant? That she'd be in better spirits with that wish coming true, and so more able to know what to do about Russ?

Why couldn't she simply ride over there, walk up to him and tell him she no longer blamed him for what he'd done? No, that didn't sound right. Tell him that she forgave him? Mari grimaced, not liking that approach, either. What she said to him had to be exactly right.

How about "I love you?" Her heart turned over as she realized the truth in those words. She did love Russ. More than she could ever love any other man. But how on earth could she walk up to him and blurt that out? Especially since she had no idea how he felt. She knew he wanted her, but that wasn't love. Maybe she'd just embarrass him.

* * *

In the days that followed she kept agonizing over how to approach Russ, and failing to solve the dilemma. Her consolation was seeing the gazebo take shape before her eyes. When it was finished and painted sparkling white, with lilac bushes planted around it, she could hardly wait for the paint to dry.

"I'll have to wait till next spring for the lilacs to flower," she told Willa as they stood admiring the octagonal building.

"I told Stan to pick up some lilac blooms from the florist," Willa said. "If we're going to have company tonight, we need flowers."

"Company? Who's coming?"

"Stan invited Russ for dinner. He's going to cook some of his famous ribs on the outside grill."

"He invited Russ?" Mari echoed.

"Why not?"

"Well, I—because I—"

"You never got around to inviting him. That's why Stan went ahead and did."

Hurrying into the house, Mari flung open her closet and stared at what it contained. Almost all of what she thought of as her New York clothes were back at Grandpa Joe's place. Which was okay, since she didn't want to wear anything dressy. Casual, but not jeans, she decided. Finally she found the white skirt she'd bought in Mackinac. It might be mid-September, but it was warm, and besides, Nevada didn't follow the no white after Labor Day rule. She pulled out a lilac, short-sleeved silk shirt she hadn't worn in a long time. Perfect.

Now if only she could come up with what to say to Russ she'd be all set.

As evening approached, Mari decided she'd never felt so nervous in her life. It was going to be all she could do to keep her cool and make semi-intelligent conversation, much less make any kind of confession to him.

As Russ waited for Stan in the café they'd agreed on, he tried once more to figure out just what the old rancher had in mind. Why this secrecy, when in a couple hours he'd be at their place for dinner?

He greeted Stan's arrival with relief, asking, "What's the deal?"

"You a gambling man?" Stan asked.

Russ started to shake his head, then said, "Stocks."

"Yeah, guess you might call the stock market a gamble. So that means you'll be up for this."

Russ raised his eyebrows.

"I figure maybe that builder of yours let you in on the fact that one of his men was throwing up a gazebo for Mari. She's always wanted one."

"I know."

"Willa claims you told Mari some kind of Indian tale about a guy coming down from the evening star to rescue a maiden. Sounded kind of peculiar to me, but it gave Willa this harebrained notion you can take or leave...."

After Stan left him, Russ drove back to his property smiling. Whether or not Willa and Stan's plan worked, it should be an interesting evening.

When he arrived at the Crowley Ranch that evening for dinner, Russ thought Mari seemed as stiff as he'd ever seen her. Not that she was anything but courteous. Something, he knew, was seriously troubling her. Stan's barbecued ribs were delicious and so were Willa's additions to the meal. By the time they finished and the table was cleared, twilight had set in. It would soon be dark.

"I got something I want to show you in the barn," Stan said to Russ.

"Let's go sit in the gazebo while they're fooling around with whatever 'tis," he heard Willa urge Mari as he left with Stan.

He noticed the padded seats inside the gazebo and the bushes around it as he passed by on the way to the barn. "Those look like lilacs," he remarked to Stan.

"Yeah, Willa'll be putting out those lilac blooms I got from the florist. Only way we can get the smell of lilacs in the gazebo this time of the year." He stopped and pointed. "There's what I rigged up. Lucky that Mari was so busy getting dolled up she didn't even notice."

Since he was about to risk his neck on it, Russ studied the contraption carefully. A thick cable ran from the barn roof to the top of the gazebo. Attached to it was a sort of chairlike apparatus on a pulley.

"Borrowed it from the casino people. They use it in their theater sometimes. Never killed an actor yet, they told me." Stan grinned.

How about a lawyer turned horse breeder? Russ wondered. He shifted his gaze to the sky above the barn roof, where Venus was just coming into view, bright and shining. The goddess of love. He took a deep breath. To tell the truth, what scared him was what Mari's reaction might be, not sliding down the cable.

After a few minutes in the gazebo, Willa got up and said to Mari, "I'm going in to brew us some tea. Enough for the men if they want any. Stan's got to liking it lately. You stay here. I'll only be a couple minutes.''

Mari nodded, rising and leaning back against one of the gazebo posts. For some reason Willa had insisted on bringing the lilacs that had been the table centerpiece out to the gazebo with them, and now the scent surrounded her, reminding her of what she ought to forget. Russ had been pleasant enough at dinner, but distant, at least where she was concerned. Did he care for her at all?

Well, of course he did physically, but otherwise?

She sighed, glancing up at the sky, where she looked every night since Willa had told her Venus was the evening star. There it was, brilliant in the darkening sky. She frowned. What was that wire stretching from the barn roof?

Before she could move to the opposite side to get a better look, she gasped. A dark mass was sliding down the wire—what in heaven's name?

She gaped in astonishment as the object stopped at the rail and Russ extracted himself, boosting himself over the rail into the gazebo.

He spread his arms and intoned, ''Fair maiden, I come from the evening star. Will you be mine?''

Totally taken aback, she managed to pull herself together enough to whisper, ''Yes.''

A second later she was in his arms, being thoroughly kissed.

After a time, he whispered in her ear. ''I have a feeling we might have interested observers.''

Then she realized he must have had assistance in setting all this up. Stan's. And probably Willa's, too. After all, hadn't Willa told her to get the gazebo built before she did anything else? But Russ was the one who'd come down to her from the evening star. Russ, the incurable romantic. Her Russ.

''I love you,'' she murmured.

''I should hope so, if you're going to be my wife.''

She pulled away to gaze into his face, only a blur in the gathering darkness. ''Wife?''

''Didn't you say yes?''

She had, in fact, but when he'd asked if she'd be his, she hadn't realized it was a proposal. ''Do you love me?'' she blurted.

''Egads and gadzooks, fair maiden, do you think I'd have risked coming down that thing otherwise?''

''You haven't said it outright.''

''Can't honestly say I loved you at first sight.

I think it crept up on me somewhere between the cupola and the foggy boat ride. '' He gathered her to him again and whispered in her ear, ''I love you, fair maiden, and if I didn't feel sure we have an audience, I'd show you just how much.''

''Too bad we're not in your tree house,'' she murmured.

Releasing her, he said, ''That's easily enough remedied.'' He grasped her hand and pulled her down the steps of the gazebo to the 4X4 he'd parked in the yard.

Mari hugged her happiness to herself during the ride to Russ's ranch, where he swerved onto a barely discernible track leading to the creek. In the dark they climbed the ladder into the tree house. When he lit a lantern, its dim glow lent a romantic ambiance to the interior.

''I've been sleeping here,'' he said, indicating a mat where a neatly folded blanket lay. ''Something I've always wanted to do.'' He put his arms around her, holding her slightly away from him. ''I never dreamed I'd be making love to the most desirable woman in the world in my tree house, though.''

Cupola, boat cabin in the fog, now a tree house, she thought. I'm going to marry a true romantic, who just happens to be the man I love.

Then he kissed her and her mind went on hold while her body took over, signaling what it needed, answered by his.

Both were too keyed up with escalating passion to wait. Clothes scattered this way and that until they lay flesh to flesh on the mat, his caresses driving her wild. When they joined together, their journey to the summit was so indescribably wonderful that tears filled Mari's eyes.

Holding her afterward, Russ said, "You're crying. What's wrong?"

"Nothing's wrong," she said huskily. "The tears are because I'm so happy what's between us has turned out to be love."

He leaned over and brushed his lips over hers. "Surprised the hell out of me to be ambushed by love."

"I should never have doubted you."

"Why not? I doubted myself. What changed your mind?"

"Willa showed me the right way to look at it. If I was the reason you and your father reconciled, then I'm glad you did what he asked of you."

"You can't imagine how I hated being a spy."

"But look what happened because of it."

"Yeah. I got you, babe. And if you think I ever mean to let you go, you're badly mistaken. I never thought I'd trust another woman after Denise, but you're nothing like her. I regret suspecting you might be an impostor. All along, though, something kept telling me you were anything but. I love you, Mari—how could I help it?''

"So you'll never let me go?" she teased.

"Not in a million years."

He pulled her closer, his lips claimed hers, and she felt his arousal even as heat rose in her again. "You couldn't lose me if you tried," she told him while she could still think well enough to form words.

Then there was nothing but Russ.

Chapter Fifteen

When Mari flew back to New York, Russ was with her, since they'd decided to deliver their news in person.

"I know Grandpa Joe likes you, but are you sure your father won't mind having me as a daughter-in-law?" she asked as they settled into the limo waiting for them at Kennedy Airport. "I once thought of him as the enemy, because I felt he was."

"Not anymore, he isn't. In fact I'll bet he'll wind up taking all the credit for us getting together."

She smiled at Russ. "I don't care. We know better. Oh, I'll admit your father set up the situation, but we could have detested each other on sight. Besides, that leaves Uncle Stan out of the equation. He was the instigator."

"My hunch is your grandfather will take over the moment we make the announcement. The odds are we won't have much say in the wedding plans. Do you mind?"

Actually, she did. She didn't answer right away, trying to decide how strongly she felt about having a say in her own wedding. Was this where she should take a stand, as Willa had advised?

"It'll be elaborate, you can count on that," Russ said. "No little chapel and a few guests. I'll go along with whatever you want—as long as your first requirement is as soon as possible."

Yes, she wanted it soon. That was one thing she'd fight for.

"How about you?" she asked. "You once told me how you disliked all the frills when you married Denise. "

"I've since wondered how much was the frills and how much a feeling I might be making a mistake. While I do prefer simplicity, I wouldn't dream of throwing cold water on Joe's plans."

She nodded. "He missed his daughter's wedding. We owe him one, I guess."

Since Russ had called his dad and asked him to be at Joe's apartment when they arrived, both men were waiting when the housekeeper let Russ and Mari in the door.

"Come to ask my permission, have you?" Joe asked Russ after greeting them both.

Mari saw Russ blink, and realized that hadn't crossed his mind. But he recovered fast. "Yes, sir. Since your granddaughter has given me the honor of agreeing to be my wife, I trust you'll give us your blessing."

Joe glanced at his old friend. "Think I should, Lou?"

Mari found herself holding her breath as Lou Simon's gaze rested on her.

"I'm not wrong often," Lou began.

Joe gave a disbelieving snort, stopping him momentarily.

"I'll admit I was not only wrong this time," Lou continued, "but before, with my son, as well." Still focused on Mari, he said, "I hope you'll overlook my meddling. As with most good intentions, mine went down the wrong road." He clapped Russ on the shoulder. "You were right all the time. Think about it, though, you two. My blunder did result in you getting acquainted.''

Mari couldn't help glancing at Russ, who winked at her.

''I take it that speech was lawyerese for me to go ahead,'' Joe commented with a grin. ''Would've anyway. Couldn't have picked a better man for you, my dear. See to it, Russ, that you make my girl happy.''

Mari gave her grandfather a hug as Russ said, ''I intend to try my best.''

''I'm glad you like horses,'' Lou told her, straight-faced, but she saw the teasing in his green eyes, so like his son's.

''Well, now, we have a wedding to plan,'' Joe said, rubbing his hands together. ''Not New York, no. Mackinac Island, that's the ticket.''

Nevada hadn't even crossed his mind, Mari realized. Thinking it over, she decided Stan and Willa would really enjoy coming to the island, and so would her other friends. She wouldn't argue about that.

''We want it to be soon, Grandfather,'' she said.

''Have to be. October's the end of the season there. I'll get my secretary cracking on the details first thing in the morning.''

"Getting late, Son," Lou reminded Russ. "Time to call it a day."

After Russ and his dad left, Joe said to Mari, "You must be tired. I'll let you go to bed. Tell me first, though, are you sure he's the man you want above all others?"

Remembering how Isabel had wound up running off with her choice, Mari picked her words carefully. "I'm so glad you approve of Russ, because I couldn't possibly think of marrying anyone else."

Her grandfather smiled at her. "The boy's got guts, standing up to that rock-ribbed old man of his. Like to see that in a kid. Made it on his own. You chose well. I only wish Isabel..." His words trailed off and he sighed.

Mari waited a moment before saying, "My mother was still a teenager. I remember being that age and how little sense I had then."

Nodding, Joe said, "I didn't have the patience I needed to deal with my daughter. Not that she was right about Morrison, but I should have found a way for the two of us to trust one another long before she met him." He looked at Mari. "Do you trust me, my dear?"

It was late, he must be tired and she knew she was. Though he'd offered an opening for her to discuss how she felt about living her own life, she didn't think this was the right time.

"You've given me no reason to mistrust you," she said, "so of course I trust you." Rising from her chair, she crossed to kiss him on the cheek and added, "I feel you're my friend as well as my grandfather."

On that high note, they both retired for the evening.

A week later, Mari reflected ruefully that Russ had been right. All the wedding preparations had been taken out of her hands. Natalie, Grandpa Joe's secretary, informed her that she'd be responsible only for making out the bride's guest list and, of course, choosing her own wedding gown.

Neither task took much time but, unfortunately, the gown fittings kept her in the city, preventing her from joining Russ. The end of the tourist season on Mackinac was rapidly coming to a close, so he was busy supervising the transportation of many of his Blues off the island back to his Lower Michigan farm. He called often to say he missed her and that their wedding day couldn't come soon enough to suit him. But hearing his voice on the phone wasn't the same as being with him.

Grandpa Joe took her to lunch in Manhattan a week before they were due to leave for the island. Apparently he sensed how she felt because, over their salads, he asked, "Everything all right—other than the missing Russ?"

"I do miss him terribly," Mari admitted. She hesitated, then added, "I have to tell you I'm beginning to feel totally useless. I may be the bride, but I'm no more than a figurehead."

"I want you to have all the trimmings, an occasion you'll remember all your life. I got cheated out of my daughter's wedding, but you've given me a second chance, and I intend to make use of it. This'll be a Haskell wedding, my dear."

A Haskell wedding, meaning an elaborate show. She supposed maybe that was what was expected of Joe Haskell, and he didn't intend to disappoint anyone. Besides, she *was* a Haskell, after all. He looked forward to this so eagerly she wouldn't dream of letting him down by telling him she'd be satisfied with less. A lot less. All she really wanted was Russ.

Trying not to count the days until they'd be together again, Mari concentrated on getting to know her grandfather better. By the time they were ready to leave for the island, she truly felt they'd become friends. Still, when they landed on

Mackinac, she still hadn't found the right way to express how increasingly stifled she felt.

The October day was flawless, the sky so achingly blue it hurt to look at it. "Indian summer," Joe said as they settled into the carriage to be driven to the cottage. "Best time of the year."

"I've never known an Indian summer," she confessed. "Nevada doesn't have them."

"They come in October after a spell of cold fall weather that hints at winter's arrival. The days turn warm again, with the trees all in brilliant color, so beautiful. It's a gift given to those of us brave enough to live where the winters are long and cold." He grinned at her. "But I'm not crazy enough to spend winters in the north."

"Northern Nevada doesn't get a long winter," she said. "Around Lake Tahoe they get a lot of snow, though."

"Tahoe," Joe repeated. "Beautiful lake."

"Do you think Russ and his father are on the island yet?" she asked, so eager to see Russ she could hardly contain herself.

"Should be coming in today, anyway."

At the cottage, to Mari's pleased surprise, she found that in the study, the portrait of her mother, now in a beautiful frame, was hanging on the wall opposite Yvonne's.

"Thank you, Grandpa Joe," she said.

"Isabel should have been there all along," he said gruffly. "My stupidity."

In the early afternoon, Willa and Uncle Stan arrived. Mari barely had time to hug Stan before her grandfather bore him off "to get acquainted with a real Nevadan."

Mari and Willa retreated to the upstairs sitting room with a tea tray.

"Fancy place," Willa said.

Mari nodded, sighing. "The wedding will be, too."

Willa eyed her. "'Tis your grandfather's way of trying to make up for lost years. Best to humor him."

"I am. He deserves to have his way."

Willa set down her cup, leaned forward and tapped Mari on the knee. "For the wedding, yes. But not for everything, gal. Sometime soon you best speak your mind." Sitting back, she said, "Right about now, I could do with a lay-down. Riding in those jet planes tires a body more'n a hard day's work."

Mari escorted Willa to her bedroom, then retrieved the tea tray. She was going down the back stairs to bring it to the kitchen when she heard the doorbell. Though she knew Pauline would answer the summons, she hurriedly set the tray on a counter and all but ran toward the entry, hoping it was Russ. Her heart sank when she saw Pauline greeting a young blond woman. Where was Russ?

Pauline turned, saying, "Mari, this is Russ's sister, Amy, all the way from California."

"The bride!" the blonde exclaimed, stepping forward to give Mari a hug. "I know you must be busy, but I couldn't resist coming over to meet you."

Except for her green eyes, Amy looked nothing like Russ, being petite as well as blond.

"I can tell by your expression that you're wondering if I'm a changeling, someone who got into the Simon family by mistake" Amy said. "They tell me I'm a throwback to our great-grandmother, who, scandal of scandals, was a chorus girl on Broadway when great-grandpa met her. I've always thought he must have been a true romantic."

"Like Russ," Mari said, already sure she was going to like Amy.

Amy's eyes widened. "Russ? You can't be speaking of my big brother."

"He really is. It isn't every man who'd come down from the Evening Star to rescue an unhappy maiden."

"Russ did what? I think we have to talk about this."

"Upstairs?" Mari suggested.

"Oh, yes, I love that little sitting room."

By the time Mari finished the story, Amy was helpless with laughter. When she sobered enough to talk, she said, "You know about Denise?"

Mari nodded.

"Denise always claimed my brother didn't have any money sense or even the romantic soul that should go with someone who didn't care about a career. He sure picked the wrong gal the first time. Which is what I told him."

"He mentioned that."

"Obviously you bring out the best in Russ. Thank heaven. He hasn't looked so happy in years." Amy's expression was so wistful that Mari wondered momentarily about Russ's sister's life.

Unable to wait any longer, Mari asked, "Is Russ on the island?"

"Not yet. We expect him any time, though," Amy rose from her chair. "I'll run along so you can get back to those last minute tasks that always pop up."

Mari smiled, not mentioning that actually she

had nothing to do because it was all being done for her.

As it turned out, Russ barely got to the island in time for the wedding rehearsal the next day. What with having to meet those of the wedding party she didn't already know, Mari scarcely had a chance to say hello to him before they were swept into rehearsal.

It wasn't until the rehearsal dinner Russ managed to sneak Mari away long enough to satisfy their longing to hold each other, but they had little chance for anything more than a few kisses before they were discovered.

"We should have eloped," he said as they were surrounded by well-wishers again.

At the moment, she felt the same way, even though she knew she couldn't have done that to Grandpa Joe. Not after Isabel.

Russ couldn't get out of the bachelor party planned for him, so Mari didn't see him again that evening. The next day, appointments for hair and nails filled her morning and then it was time to get ready. Her bridal gown was the simplest she'd been able to find.

"Elegant," Amy told her. "Suits you beautifully. You aren't a frilly person."

Since this was Mari's own evaluation of herself, she warmed even more to Amy.

"Russ's gift to the bride?" Amy asked, lifting from a velvet box an exquisite gold pin with a lilac blossom enameled on it.

Mari smiled. "He knows I love lilacs."

"Like our mother did. Hold still and I'll pin it in place."

It was as though Amy's presence grounded her, because after Amy left with the other bridesmaids, Mari's grasp of her surroundings became less and less real, though she did know that Grandpa Joe was on one side of her and Uncle Stan on the other as she walked up the aisle toward Russ, at the altar.

The actual ceremony passed in a blur. The only clear moment for her was when Russ looked into her eyes and said, as though to her alone, "I do."

The reception was, of course, held at the Grand Hotel, another whirlwind of people, all wishing them well. Somewhere in the middle of it, Grandpa Joe separated her from Russ, taking her into a small room where the two of them were alone.

"Thought I'd discuss some of my plans for you," he began.

His words brought her out of her daze, Willa's

advice foremost in her mind. Now Mari told herself. Now is the time. She held up her hand.

"Grandfather, please. I need to say something first. I love you and want to be with you as much as I can be, but I also want to live my own life. I have to. You know what happened to Russ and his father. I wouldn't ever wish that on you and me, so you can't go on arranging my life for me as though it's a—well, an occasion like a Haskell wedding. Russ has a horse ranch in Nevada now and I want to help him with it, which means I'll be spending a lot of time in Nevada. I hope you can understand." She looked at him apprehensively.

He nodded. "You're a Haskell, all right. Takes one to know one. You keep right on standing up for yourself, my dear. I did learn from the fiasco with Isabel, but we Haskells just can't resist trying to order everyone's life. As it happens, I've always wanted a place near Tahoe—they tell me it's a great sailing lake."

"Tahoe?" she repeated.

"Not far from that ranch Russ bought, is it?"

"Thirty miles or so," she managed to say.

"That's an easy distance for visiting back and forth. Of course, I'll expect you to bring the children to Mackinac for at least part of the summer."

"Grandpa Joe," she protested. "Russ and I are hardly married."

He grinned at her. "So?"

She reached out and hugged him, understanding that he was offering a compromise. If he could, so could she. "Your great-grandchildren will love the island as much as I do," she said.

He led her back into the milling mass of guests, where Russ promptly found her and engineered their escape. When they were safely in the buggy, riding away from the hotel, he said, "What did Joe want?"

"Nothing much," she said. "Only a promise to let the children spend summers on Mackinac."

"Children? Ours?" He drew her into his arms and murmured, "In that case, why keep him waiting?"

Epilogue

"Gapa," two-year-old Elias insisted loudly. "Gapa do."

Mari shook her head and looked at her grandfather. "I guess you'll have to put his boots on."

Joe chuckled. "Good to see the Haskell spirit handed down." He reached for the boots.

Mari rolled her eyes. "The combination of the terrible twos and the Haskell spirit can be daunting, not to say tiresome."

"I suppose that's why you're having another."

Since she barely showed even a bulge, Mari frowned. "Russ told you."

Shaking his head, Joe said, "Got eyes in my head, haven't I? I may be old, but I still know what's going on." He pulled the second boot onto his great-grandson's foot. "Okay, buddy, let's get cracking."

"Buddy," Elias repeated, obviously enchanted with the word. "Buddy, buddy."

"That's what we are, you and me," Grandpa Joe told him. "Buddies. Let's go see your birthday present."

Feeling the warmth of the May Nevada sun, Mari followed them from the ranch house to where the gift—a child's dapple-gray pony— waited. The scent of the lilacs Russ had planted around the house drifted on the breeze.

"Horsie," Elias said, marching up to the animal.

"No—pony," Joe corrected. "Your pony."

"Horsie."

"Pony." He handed Elias a slice of apple. "Feed the pony."

Elias, who'd been fearlessly feeding his father's big draft horses since he was old enough to understand what to do, held out the piece of apple on his palm, and the pony promptly snaffled it up.

"Now he knows you're his buddy," Joe said.

Elias's green eyes looked from the pony to his

great-grandfather and back. "Buddy," he said, pointing at the animal. "Up."

"A rider already, are you?" Joe said, lifting him onto the pony's saddled back and holding him there. He glanced at Mari. "I guess he likes his pony."

"No po'y," Elias announced. "Buddy."

"Okay, that's his name," Joe said. "Good choice."

With Grandpa Joe holding her son, Mari walked Buddy around the paddock, chuckling to herself at the interchange between the old man and the little boy. She eyed Elias's brown hair, so close to Joe's gray head, and thought how good it was to see her grandfather enjoying him. She marveled at his patience with the child—more than she had sometimes.

How wonderful that Elias could grow up having not only Great-grandpa Joe around but Grandpa Stan and Grandpa Lou as well. Willa, too. He was surrounded by people who loved him.

Finally Elias tired of riding the pony, and Joe took him off to the creek to look for tadpoles. As one of the ranch hands led the pony away to unsaddle him, from behind Mari, Russ said, "How did the riding session go?"

She turned and he put an arm around her.

"More importantly, how are you and our next one doing?" he asked.

"Joe noticed."

"He doesn't miss much."

"Elias has already named his new pony Buddy. When we get to Mackinac next month, I just hope Grandpa Joe hasn't already bought a snowbird for him and is planning on teaching him to sail."

Russ chuckled, then leaned to whisper in her ear, "Speaking of boats, when we get to Mackinac, how about the two of us sailing into a patch of Lake Huron fog?"

She smiled impishly. "Mackinac Island is a month away—do you really want to wait that long?"

The flash in his green eyes clearly showed her he didn't. So did the urgency in the quick kiss he gave her before turning her toward the house. He paused to break off a lilac bloom and hand it to her before they went inside and up the stairs. She held the flowerets to her heart, the sweet scent reminding her of the love they would always share.

* * * * *

CALL THE ONES YOU LOVE OVER THE HOLIDAYS!

Save $25 off future book purchases when you buy any four Harlequin® or Silhouette® books in October, November and December 2001,

PLUS

receive a phone card good for 15 minutes of long-distance calls to anyone you want in North America!

WHAT AN INCREDIBLE DEAL!

Just fill out this form and attach 4 proofs of purchase (cash register receipts) from October, November and December 2001 books, and Harlequin Books will send you a coupon booklet worth a total savings of $25 off future purchases of Harlequin® and Silhouette® books, AND a 15-minute phone card to call the ones you love, anywhere in North America.

Please send this form, along with your cash register receipts as proofs of purchase, to:
In the USA: Harlequin Books, P.O. Box 9057, Buffalo, NY 14269-9057
In Canada: Harlequin Books, P.O. Box 622, Fort Erie, Ontario L2A 5X3
Cash register receipts must be dated no later than December 31, 2001.
Limit of 1 coupon booklet and phone card per household.
Please allow 4-6 weeks for delivery.

I accept your offer! Please send me my coupon booklet and a 15-minute phone card:

Name: _____

Address: _____ City: _____

State/Prov.: _____ Zip/Postal Code: _____

Account Number (if available): _____

---

097 KJB DAGL
PHQ4012

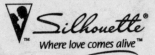